I0716401

Crafting Disorder

PONDEROSA PINES MYSTERIES
BOOK TWO

REGINA WELLING

ERIN LYNN

Willow Hill
BOOKS

Copyright © 2015 by ReGina Welling

ISBN: 978-1-953044-18-1

All rights reserved.

No part of this book may be reproduced in any form or by any electronic or mechanical means, including information storage and retrieval systems, without written permission from the author, except for the use of brief quotations in a book review.

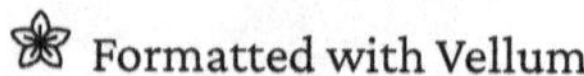 Formatted with Vellum

Contents

Chapter 1 — 1
Chapter 2 — 17
Chapter 3 — 37
Chapter 4 — 49
Chapter 5 — 56
Chapter 6 — 62
Chapter 7 — 76
Chapter 8 — 82
Chapter 9 — 91
Chapter 10 — 95
Chapter 11 — 107
Chapter 12 — 116
Chapter 13 — 125
Chapter 14 — 139
Chapter 15 — 154
Chapter 16 — 163
Chapter 17 — 171
Chapter 18 — 179
Chapter 19 — 186
Chapter 20 — 192
Chapter 21 — 199
Chapter 22 — 210
Chapter 23 — 218
Chapter 24 — 225
Chapter 25 — 232
Chapter 26 — 236
Chapter 27 — 243

Chapter 28   258
Chapter 29   278
Chapter 30   283
Excerpt from Caught in the Frame   293
A Free Story for You   300
Other Books   306

Crafting Disorder

Chapter 1

"I blame you." Chloe LaRue brandished a fist-sized pumpkin at her best friend, EV Torrence. "I know I never agreed to this." She added the pumpkin to the growing pile in the back of EV's rickety pickup bed.

"You love this kind of crap. You live for decorating the town for the 'hoopla of the month'."

"Yeah, but not at the butt-crack of dawn." Chloe's clenched teeth clipped the words short.

"Can't have the kiddies losing faith in the pumpkin fairy, now, can we?" EV's hand snapped up to catch the tiny pumpkin flying toward her head.

"Pumpkin fairy." Chloe snorted. If it weren't so early, the mental image of the pair of them in tutus and wings, with wands that disgorged orange globes, would have made her laugh out loud. "Too bad there's no coffee fairy." If Chloe had her way, morning people would all fall off the face of the planet and leave her in peace until a respectable hour. EV would be the first to go. She'd miss her best friend, but at least the mornings would be quiet.

EV flipped the driver's seat forward to reveal a small cooler—one of those that plugs into the cigarette lighter, and can also keep things warm--and pulled out two thermal coffee cups. Chloe nearly pounced on hers, decorated in a pink paisley pattern. "You were holding out on me."

"It's the good stuff. Perked in that old enamel camp pot."

Chloe had emptied the cup and returned it to the cooler before enough caffeine coursed through her system to burn away the fog.

Even at this ridiculous hour, the town of Ponderosa Pines captivated Chloe with its rustic honesty. What passed for downtown was little more than a short street lined with several locally owned businesses. Each building sported either solar panels or small wind turbines—sometimes both—a familiar sight in a town dedicated to eco-friendly, green living.

This mid-September morning, the leaves, taking on the tints of autumn, looked as though their edges had been airbrushed with color. Pale morning sun drew diamond sparkles in the heavy dew that lay on each leafy tip. The pale morning sky that hovered over the town, Chloe knew, would darken to a perfect, robin's-egg blue over the next hour or so. She sighed and bent to set another small pumpkin into place in a window box full of cheerful mums in full bloom. EV was right: she did feel like the pumpkin fairy, leaving her bounty to decorate the world. The fanciful notion surprised her. What had EV put in that coffee, anyway? Goofy juice?

Chloe's blond hair spilled out in soft waves from under a bright pink knit hat, framing a heart-shaped face, and full, pouting lips. In the three years since she had returned to the Pines, Chloe had exchanged her jet-set attire for a style more conducive to country living. A puffy vest over a long-sleeved, thermal tee kept her warm in the crisp autumn air, and form-fitting jeans tucked into well-worn faux-leather boots completed the ensemble. Years of traveling the globe had netted Chloe a myriad of colorful accessories, which she used to add a little something extra to every outfit. Today, the vibrant hat—along with a matching scarf and hand-knit boot cuffs—melded the two styles seamlessly.

Looking around the small town of Ponderosa

Pines, Chloe once again felt grateful that she had made the inspired decision to settle back into provincial life. Surrounded by friends she considered family, Chloe felt a swelling of happiness and contentment; it would be hard to pick any single thing to be appreciative of this Thanksgiving.

For the first time in her fifty-three years of life, EV took little pleasure in getting the town ready for another event. Since the recent deaths of brothers Luther and Evan Plunkett—one the result of murder—her shining town felt a shade darker; as if the thinnest haze had settled over everything like a layer of tarnish on fine silver.

The town mantra of *nothing bad ever happens in Ponderosa Pines* had been proved wrong in the worst possible way. Maybe they would have to switch to *Ponderosa Pines: it's been ~~eternity~~ 59 days since our last murder.* That thought brought a wry smile to her angular face.

Now that things were getting back to normal—the Ponderosa Pines version of it anyway—maybe the pall would lift, and take some of the load on her shoulders with it. Being considered a suspect in the murder—even by a small contingent of townspeople

—had weighed more heavily on her than she wanted to admit to anyone.

This decorating project should have been a distraction, but so far, fell far short of its goal. Her mind was still running through a laundry list of woes when she heard Chloe yell, "Look out!"

Half a second too late, she glanced up to watch an orange boulder of imminent pumpkin death rolling toward her from the top of the pile. It was too late to pivot, so the best she could do was try to catch the thing. It was also too late to calculate the effects of speed and momentum. All she had time to do was pinwheel her arms before it slammed into her like a bowling ball taking down a pin. Taking two stumbling steps backwards to compensate for the force of the blow, EV tripped over a pile of corn stalks and landed flat out, pumpkin and all, right at Dalton Burnsoll's feet.

How humiliating.

Chloe was there in an instant to help Dalton lift the pumpkin off EV's chest.

"Are you all right? Oh, my God, EV." Chloe grabbed EV's hand while Dalton fell to his knees and ran his fingers over her gently, checking for broken bones.

EV threw the other arm over her face and began to shake, while Chloe and Dalton exchanged concerned looks.

"You have to tell me where it hurts." Dalton urged as he reached for his phone to call Doc Talbot.

"I think I broke my dignity; help me up. There's an ear of corn in my...I'm being goosed!" This time her giggle was audible, and Dalton slid his phone back into his pocket.

She made quite a picture; all six feet of her lean frame draped over several stacks of bundled corn stalks, sable hair disordered from the fall.

Reaching down with both hands, Dalton pulled EV up until they stood eye to eye. Growing up together meant that they were well beyond the awkward getting-to-know-you phase when it came to dating. Even so, EV had proved a tough nut to crack. One date had barely put a dent in her armor, but Dalton knew she had forged it in the fire of a serious romantic disappointment. He was no stranger to that kind of pain himself, having recently divorced, but he was determined to try again. With EV. The challenge lie in convincing her to give up her loner status and take a chance on him.

As though she had just realized she was holding

hands with Dalton in the middle of town, EV snatched hers back and, in doing so, bumped the tailgate to send another large gourd rolling. "Christine's trying to pick up the spare." EV chortled

Chloe's heart had barely slowed to a normal rhythm. Another round of 'bowling for best friends' was not on her list of fun things to do, so she slammed the tailgate shut and wagged a finger at her friend.

"Better watch it, old woman; you could break a hip." Chloe's wiggling finger shook a little from the after-effects of the fear that had also bleached the color from her face. Whether EV found the situation humorous or not, Chloe wasn't quite ready for jokes.

"Christine?" Dalton always felt like he ran a step behind with these two.

"The truck." When his brow remained furrowed, Chloe elaborated, "Christine—the car from the Stephen King novel—it came to life and started killing people... "

Dalton shook his head, tuning back to EV, who was brushing herself off and pointedly averting her gaze from his.

Deep crinkles framed the corners of a pair of intelligent eyes, and proved that Dalton laughed often. Dark hair with enough curl to be unruly—and enough gray at the temples to mark his fifty-three years—fell messily over his tanned forehead. Handsome, trustworthy, and solid—qualities EV appreciated, and Dalton had them in spades—despite being determined not to get into a relationship, she couldn't seem to put a damper on her attraction to him.

"I'm fine." She shook her hips to prove it. "Tell me you're not wishing you had that on camera. You'd have it up on YouTube before I hit the ground." Chloe's lips twitched. She would have done no such thing. She'd have at least waited until she knew EV was okay before she posted the video.

As Chloe finished tying a bundle of corn stalks around the base of the street lamp out front, Rhonda Erickson turned the lock to open The Mudbucket, Ponderosa Pine's lone coffee shop. Another jolt of caffeine and one of David's exquisite sticky rolls studded with pecans sounded perfect, so she dragged a protesting EV inside while Dalton trailed behind.

All smiles, Rhonda maneuvered her swollen belly between tables with most of her former grace; she hadn't quite progressed to the waddle stage of her pregnancy yet, but it wouldn't be long now.

"Anyone up for pumpkin spice? It's the flavor of the week."

"Ugh, no. I think we've all seen enough pumpkins for one day." Chloe answered quickly before EV started her yearly tirade over the growing number of ridiculous items flavored or scented for fall. Candles and ice cream she could handle. The richly spiced, dark orange breads, cookies, and pies would be enjoyed. She might be tempted to sample the Pop-Tarts; even the potato chips, coffees, and teas weren't the worst of it. However, when it came to vodka, buttery spread, and beef jerky—she drew the line. What pushed her over the top, though, were the marshmallows. Or, it might have been the chewing gum; or the nuts; or the chapstick—or possibly the pet cologne.

Come to think of it, Chloe didn't disagree with her; the craze was out of hand.

A very different Rhonda returned with the food than the one who had taken their order—Chloe's pecan roll was placed next to EV, while EV's turnover ended up in front of Dalton. Distracted, Rhonda started back toward the kitchen, stopped, and turned back to take a seat at the fourth chair of their table.

"Someone has been stealing from us." If she had

said aliens had landed in the town square, EV would not have been more surprised. Murder notwithstanding, nothing like this ever happened in Ponderosa Pines.

"Stealing?" EV glanced over at Chloe and Dalton to see similar looks of surprise on both their faces.

"Oh, not like money or anything, but we put an old broken table and chair outside by the back door. The next morning, it was gone." Rhonda's fingers worked nervously at the strap of her apron. "Plus, I'm sure the scrap bucket we set aside for Mr. Thompson's pigs wasn't as full this morning as I thought it was yesterday when I set it outside. We're not missing anything of value. Has anything like this happened before?"

"No, but I'm glad you told me. I'll look into it." In his capacity as Deputy, it fell to Dalton to handle these kinds of things. Since he'd taken the job, it seemed crime rates in Ponderosa Pines had skyrocketed. First a murder, now theft?

Reassured she had done the right thing, Rhonda returned to the kitchen, the bounce returned to her step.

EV scrubbed a hand over her face, knowing that somehow, whether Dalton and his temporary trainer,

Nate Harper, were on the case or not, certain residents would expect her to handle this newest mess.

As the daughter of the first owner of property in the town of Ponderosa Pines—not to mention the woman who had almost single-handedly transformed the town from a dying commune to its currently small, but thriving population—EV carried a lot of responsibility. Whenever the town needed someone to encourage growth or handle a minor crisis, they called on EV.

"It's probably some kids trying to furnish a clubhouse or something. I can ask around." Chloe suggested. She hoped it was nothing more than kids. Recycling in this town was almost a religion, so the chances of something broken hanging around long were pretty slim. Someone would have come around and asked for the table, or traded something for it if they wanted it bad enough. Either scenario was more likely than a resident stealing from another resident —even teenagers in this town followed the rules of basic etiquette and politeness.

With a new problem to think about, conversation died, and the three of them finished eating.

Forcing her mind away from this new piece of news, EV did her best to ignore Dalton's sidelong glances. She absolutely refused to process the way holding his hand earlier had felt so right, so safe. One date did not a romance make—at least not in her book. Sure enough, he brought up the subject again.

"You still owe me a night of dancing Emmalina." Dalton grinned when her eyes narrowed at hearing the name she thought was way too frou-frou to describe herself.

"What? I had a legitimate reason for canceling last week." Okay, so maybe her excuse had been flimsy. His raised eyebrow and head tilt more eloquently displayed his disbelief than Chloe's coughed, "Liar."

"Fine, pick me up tomorrow night at 7:00." EV treated Chloe to a look that promised retribution. "But for now, it's time to get back to work." She pulled a list out of her pocket, "The church and the loaner boxes are the last of it."

Some of EV's favorite innovations were the loaner boxes erected all over town. During the summer months, the boxes held books available to anyone who wanted to exchange one from home. In the winter, they held hand-knitted hats and mittens—no exchange necessary. Each loaner box was slated for decoration with corn stalks and a mix of colorful gourds and pumpkins. Festive ribbons would add the finishing touch. There were half a dozen boxes scattered across town, so EV figured it wouldn't take long to finish them up.

She could not have been more wrong.

The task started out easily enough; the first loaner box was done in a matter of minutes, but at the next, Talia Plunkett hauled EV and Chloe inside for a chat that quickly turned into a complaint session.

"I know it's only a pile of concrete blocks, but I was planning to use them to make a garden bench for my front beds. I saw the cutest one on Pinterest, and it looked so easy to make. Why on earth would someone steal something so common?"

"We'll look into it, Talia." Chloe assured her, while dragging EV out of there before Talia could detain them any longer.

Back in the truck, EV turned to Chloe. "What the hell?"

"I know. It's a Ponderosa Pines crime wave. I hope that's the last of it."

Nope, not even close.

Horis was missing a broken wheelbarrow and an ax handle.

Mr. Zellner described in excruciating detail the search for half roll of rusty, though still perfectly usable, fencing wire that should have been hanging on a nail out behind his barn. According to him, however, the kicker was the insult to the scarecrow in his cornfield. He dragged EV and Chloe out to see.

"Just look at him; he's nekkid. You ever hear of a nekkid scarecrow? It's not right. It's indecent. "What are you going to do about these kids?"

EV covered her snort with a cough and agreed to track down the most likely suspects.

Tank Daniels complained about a missing blanket he'd been using to extend the growing season of a patch of cucumbers he was ripening to the yellow stage for a batch of relish.

Ponderosa Pines residents, whatever their foibles, always pulled together in time of need. None of the missing items were valuable, and in every case would have been given willingly to anyone who had asked for them. So far, each victim appeared unaware of the other thefts, so to them it looked like an isolated incident. But when everyone started comparing notes, this had all the makings of a blowup.

EV's old truck careened to a stop in front of the Come On Inn, one of two competing bed and breakfast establishments located directly across from each other. Open House, owned by Lottie Calabrese—sister-in-law to the recently departed Luther Plunkett—remained temporarily closed while Lottie spent time with her mourning sister, Talia. In another week, Lottie planned to reopen for business. Across the road, Come On Inn, owned by Sabra Pruitt, was in full operation. Which, for Ponderosa Pines, meant she had a single lodger; some salesperson passing through for the night. All hope of getting the loaner box finished before Sabra saw them vanished when her front door flew open. Wrapped in a colorful shawl, but still wearing a pair of flip flops on her feet despite the cooling temperatures, she advanced toward EV with purposeful steps.

Chloe's quiet groan went ignored. At this rate, she would be burning the midnight oil if she wanted to get her weekly gossip column ready for editing. None of what she had heard today was particularly juicy, but breaking the news of a rash of thefts had some appeal—as long as it wouldn't hinder what she was sure was about to become a full-blown investigation.

"You'll never guess what's happened." Sabra leaned an elbow on the hood of the truck, and prepared to settle in for a good gossip session. Out of the corner of her eye, she cast a hopeful glance over the front seat, just in case EV had brought along a jar of crabapple jelly. Sabra had been trying to get EV to tell her the secret ingredient for years. Disappointed at seeing none, she turned back to say, "Someone *borrowed,*" air quotes, "one of those decorative cast iron pots I keep my plants in out front."

"Plants and all?" EV asked.

"No, I use plastic liners, so they yanked the plant right out of the pot and left it on the porch."

The headache that had been threatening since EV's fall in town bloomed into a full throb as she once again promised to look into it, and hustled Chloe out of there as quickly as possible.

"Do we have to finish this today?" Chloe wanted to go home.

"Might as well. Nothing will change between now and tomorrow." EV's tone was dry, her face set in grim lines. "Only way to deal with this is head on."

"This is true."

Chapter 2

Dalton must have left The Mudbucket and gone straight to his temporary boss and trainer, Detective Nathanial Harper, with his newfound knowledge, because EV had barely stopped at the loaner box in front of the church when the two men sauntered up. Nate kicked one of her truck tires with a frown.

"Is this thing even road legal?"

"I don't take it on the highway, if that's what you're asking, but it does well enough to drop off a few pumpkins around town. I keep it under the speed limit."

Chloe snorted. "Trust me, turtles move faster than that thing."

"Look Missy, without a load on, she'll do a good ten miles an hour." EV teased Chloe.

From the look on his face, Chloe judged Nate would like nothing more than to give EV a ticket, but since the truck had a valid—though in this case the term was debatable—inspection sticker and registration, there was nothing he could do.

Pissing off EV was probably the worst use of his time, so he let it go.

"Tell me about the missing table." Nate gave EV his best stern cop face, which had zero effect on her.

EV lifted her shoulders; played it off. "Sounds like you already know. He was there," a nod of her head indicated Dalton. "Ask him. He knows what I know."

"Don't give me that. The two of you have made at least four other stops between here and there, gossiping all the way, no doubt."

"Well, Jingle Bells to you, too, but I don't think that's quite how it goes." Dalton bit his lip to hold back a snicker sure to get him in trouble with Nate or EV—probably both.

"I never gossip." Chloe pressed a hand to her heart and put on her best innocent face. If his smirk and raised eyebrow were anything to go by, Nate wasn't buying it. EV's snort earned her a dirty look.

"Fine. We know stuff." EV paused to decide what and how much to tell him. Based on her calculations, someone was due to connect all the minor thefts any minute now. Once that happened, the poo would hit the fan with maximum velocity, and spread around town in under an hour. No sense hiding information now.

"Things have been going missing all over town. Nothing valuable, mind you. A broken table and chair; a broken wheelbarrow; some rusty old fence wire; the clothes off of Zellner's scarecrow."

Nate suppressed a small smile at that last item.

"Everyone assumes a group of kids are trying to set up some kind of clubhouse, but I'm not buying it. All the kids in town know enough to ask if they want something. This isn't normal behavior for any of them." Chloe took over while EV circled the truck and pulled out the last sheaf of corn stalks. Dalton moved to help her while they both kept an ear on the discussion going on at the front of the truck.

"Why not? If I remember correctly—and I do— we pilfered some stuff from the town gardens in our day." Nate leaned in toward Chloe, his body angled for privacy. "For those picnics in the woods." His voice turned smooth and deep.

"Shh. Don't tell any of our dirty secrets." Chloe tried to ignore the way his vocal caress touched off shivers that started down low in her belly. Those woodland trysts had been totally innocent, but there was nothing virtuous about the way he was looking at her right now—like he could slurp her up in one long gulp. The man smelled like sin—a little spicy, with a hint of wood smoke, and something else—something unidentifiable, but intensely masculine. When the warning sounds exploded like a klaxon in her head, Chloe stepped back to put some distance between them. It was too hard to think with him standing so close.

Nate stepped closer, rested a hand on the truck next to Chloe, who ducked under it and retreated to help unload the last six pumpkins that were slated to decorate the front steps of the church. She reached for the biggest one, but he plucked it effortlessly from her grasp. Chloe's eyes narrowed as she watched him lift the hefty gourd with no trouble from his injured shoulder.

Two weeks—three at the most—and he would be gone. If she wasn't careful, he'd take her heart with him when he left. Nate's post as a detective in the nearest city of any size, Portland, had netted him a torn rotator cuff; he chose to take up the post at the Pines out of necessity and obligation. He loved his hometown, but had stated—in no uncertain terms, and on more than one occasion—that he didn't have any desire to return permanently. Either you loved the Pines, or you hated it.

Tension settled into Chloe's shoulders, tightening the muscles until they felt taut as guitar strings. She schooled her expression into one of bored indifference, snatched the next largest pumpkin from the bed of the truck, and marched toward the church, leaving Nate with no choice but to follow.

"I think the air just turned cold." Dalton observed. "Any idea what that's all about?"

"Mating dance of the young and cuckoo." EV's sharp eyes hadn't missed the hurt behind Chloe's sudden tension. Stubbornness ran deep in Chloe's family; without intervention, she stood to lose out on the love of a lifetime. EV couldn't let that happen. Good thing she already had a plan.

"Speaking of dancing, you're not going to welch on me again, right?" Dalton reminded her. She'd been putting him off ever since the day Ashton Worth nearly killed himself in EV's kitchen.

"I have a corn-related injury," EV prevaricated.

"I'd be happy to kiss it and make it better."

"Dalton Burnsoll, did you really just offer to kiss my ass?" His face flamed red, but he waggled his eyebrows suggestively.

"If that's what it takes to make sure you're ready tomorrow night when I come to pick you up." He puckered up and made loud kissing noises.

EV couldn't help but laugh; the man did have a sense of humor.

The tone signaling an incoming text saved her from having to answer right away. Roger Kroger, legal representative from the neighboring town of Gilmore, would be delighted to meet her friend Chloe for dinner and drinks. EV loved it when a good plan came together.

A recent misunderstanding between the two towns had Ponderosa Pines residents under the impression the town of Gilmore was underhandedly trying to annex their town; the powers that be in Gilmore thought Ponderosa Pines was the one seeking to combine.

Someone had been playing both ends against the middle, and perpetrating a bit of extortion in the process. Unfortunately, the blackmail victim, Evan Plunkett, had been murdered for an entirely unrelated reason before he could provide any additional information that might lead to catching the blackmailer.

The furor over the town feud—that had ended up

being mostly imaginary—may have died down temporarily, but EV and Chloe agreed that there was no way this was over. Anyone willing to go to the trouble it had taken to track down Evan's deepest secret probably still had an agenda, even if his—or her—opening play had been blocked.

They could stay quiet and wait for the blackmailer's next move, or they could be proactive and learn everything they could in order to try and find him.

With Evan gone, EV figured the best way to track the mysterious blackmailer was by gaining the cooperation of someone on the inside in Gilmore. Roger fit the bill perfectly, and EV's crime-solving partner, Chloe, was the right woman to pry information out of him. Once EV filled her in on the plan.

As an added bonus, she owed Chloe a bit of payback for pushing her into that first date with Dalton, and now that that particular can of worms had strewed its wiggling contents all over her life, she would enjoy opening one for Chloe. Just to add more incentive—if the little scene she had witnessed between Chloe and Nate was anything to go by—the pair of them needed a gentle push, or maybe a ruthless shove in the right direction. A little competition might be the fastest way to accomplish that objective.

If nothing else, the fireworks would be fun to watch.

Dalton cleared his throat, calling EV's attention back to her other, more pressing, problem. Keeping Dalton relegated to the friend zone had been considerably easier before he had kissed her senseless and even Chloe had no idea exactly how much that one kiss had changed EV's opinion of him. He'd gone from an annoyance to a distraction—which sounded like it amounted to the same thing, but the two were leagues apart.

He'd given her the tingly toes, and she couldn't forget the feel of his lips or the touch of his body where he'd pulled her against him. A night of dancing presented too many opportunities for bodily contact, but she had promised, and EV never reneged on a promise.

"Okay, but if I hear the first notes of teeny-bop music, I'm out of there. Classic rock, right? Is there any place that even plays that stuff anymore?"

"Friday nights at Drifter's in Warren. We'll do dinner first?"

Hoping their friendship could survive a trip into

true date territory, she confirmed the time while, out of the corner of her eye, EV watched Chloe and Nate return for another pair of pumpkins.

"Chloe, don't forget Roger will be by tonight to pick you up for dinner."

In the middle of reaching into the truck for her final victim, Chloe stilled, flashed EV a raised eyebrow before opening her mouth to protest. In the face of EV's pointed look, Chloe covered the momentary lapse.

"I'd almost forgotten about that. Thanks for the reminder." She risked a glance at Nate, but his face had gone cop hard and unreadable.

Turning toward Dalton, "I think we should head out to Zellner's place and take a look at that naked scarecrow of his." Nate said in a voice cold enough to freeze the ears off a brass donkey. "I'll talk to *you* later, EV." His subtle emphasis of the word *you* was not lost on Chloe, who chimed in with a cheerful-sounding, "See you later, Dalton." She waited until the men were out of sight before rounding on EV.

"Tell me that was a joke. You didn't really fix me up with Roger, right? Isn't he that nerdy-looking guy from the town meeting?"

"I did. But not for the reason you're thinking."

Chloe's mind had already gotten there, though. "It's about that Gilmore business. And Evan's blackmailer. You want me to pump Roger for information."

"Well, I don't want you to pump him for anything else."

"Ha ha." A pause, "You're evil, you know that?" Chloe wasn't really mad; the idea had possibilities. EV wasn't the only one who felt the pull of untied threads. "I'll do it because we both know this isn't over. But there will be consequences." Two could play at this game.

"Whatever." EV waved a dismissive hand. "We're done here. I have chicken stew in the crockpot. You want?"

"Dumplings?"

"Naturally."

"I'm in; if you think we can get this heap back to your place before I starve to death."

"Yeah? Watch me." EV pulled a U-turn to head back home. A quarter mile down the road, she shot Chloe a glance and took a right-hand turn down an almost hidden track through the trees. What followed next had Chloe bracing herself and clutching the seat belt. EV bounced the old truck through the woods in a nearly straight line that cut the drive time in less than half, but when the truck approached an old wooden bridge with no side rails that Chloe didn't ever remember seeing, she shrieked.

"Are you crazy? You're going to kill us!"

EV hunched over the steering wheel, flashed an evil grin, slammed her foot on the gas pedal, and sped across while Chloe swore a blue streak at her.

"I'm going to kill you if we make it back in one piece."

The truck shot out of the woods a few hundred feet from EV's driveway. She whipped the wheel to park it next to the shed before looking at her watch. "And that's the record."

Once her heart rate returned to normal, Chloe decided the chicken and dumplings would be worth staying for—but EV would be getting a side of rant with hers.

"Needs more pepper," EV handed the grinder to Chloe after dusting her own bowl liberally enough to bring on a sneeze. "You really think kids are stealing stuff around town?" She asked with watering eyes.

"Not really, do you?"

"Maybe Zellner's scarecrow, as a prank. But the rest? No. Too random. I'm betting it gets worse before it gets better. Tomorrow's my day for working at the co-op; I'll probably get an earful while I'm there."

Chloe blew on a bite of dumpling to cool it before popping it in her mouth. Her eyes dropped shut in appreciation.

'Yum. What's in these? They're heavenly." Flecks of herb and vegetable studded the dough.

"Pinch of fresh sage—chopped up fine—along with some diced onions, carrots, and celery. It's a cross between stuffing and dumplings."

"Worth almost getting killed on the way here."

EV smirked, but chose not to answer the insult to her driving.

While the stew in her bowl cooled enough to eat without burning her tongue, EV jotted down a list of missing items on a pastel purple legal pad. She could see no pattern, other than that most were unusable, and had been slated for recycling.

After puzzling over it for another minute, she pushed the list aside. Tilting her head, she observed Chloe until the other woman put down her spoon, and asked, "What?"

"We should come up with a strategy for dealing with Roger."

"How about you go on the date—that's a strategy that works for me."

"Meow. Cougar on the prowl? I don't think I'm his type, but I do think that if you vamp him too hard, you're going to open Pandora's Box."

"Truth. I'll be careful, and you can trust me to get the skinny—whatever skinny there is to get, anyway." Time to change the subject. "What are you thinking about these thefts?"

"I'm thinking we have another case to solve."

"Yes, please, another vodka-soda, light on the vodka. How about you, Roger, would you like a refill on your rum and coke?" Chloe purred, shooting Roger a flirtatious look from beneath her eyelashes.

"Um, yes, absolutely." He stammered, draining the dregs of his last drink before handing his glass to the waitress. *About one more and I'm golden,* thought Chloe with an internal smirk. It wasn't that Roger wasn't a nice guy, but what kind of man ordered coconut-flavored rum in front of a woman on the first date? A whiskey and coke? Sure. A long island iced tea? Perfectly acceptable. Girlie drinks, however, should be saved for a tropical vacation. Or for lazy Sundays watching Netflix with your steady girlfriend. Though Chloe did admire his total lack of self-consciousness, she felt a pang of guilt for being judgmental—and for accepting a date with an ulterior motive. Still, she had a goal to accomplish, and accomplish it she would.

"Tell me about yourself, Roger." Chloe hoped he wouldn't need too much prodding before letting slip some useful information.

By the time the food arrived—Chloe's salmon Caesar salad looked as delicious as Roger's fish and chips—Chloe had learned that Roger held a degree in architecture, was an avid camper, and loved classic '80's movies. Upon further inspection, he wasn't that bad looking either, in a corporate sort of way. He sure looked good on paper, but Chloe wasn't getting the *tinglies* like she did when a certain someone was around.

"So how did an architect from Gilmore wind up at a Ponderosa Pines town meeting, anyway?" Chloe gently pressed for information.

"Well, my side project is flipping houses. I deal with the planning, and my partner does the remodeling. We've been delving into more eco-friendly materials and methods. It's why I volunteered to attend your town meeting; I was curious." He finished, looking somewhat sheepish.

"Ah-ha, ulterior motives!" Chloe exclaimed with a genuine smile. "If you ever need a brain to pick, please ask...though our methods aren't always the most flashy or hi-tech." Roger's eyes lit up at the offer, and Chloe realized she might want to scale it back a notch, lest he develop a hard-core crush she'd have to nix.

"Tell me the real story behind Ponderosa Pines. I've heard some crazy rumors, but I don't tend to put much stock into gossip." Chloe had to choke back a laugh at that; her job as secret gossip columnist for the Pines' weekly newsletter, *The Pine Cone*, made innuendo her business. Nobody in town, save for her editor, Wesley, and her best friend, EV, knew she held the position. The secrecy created a buzz, making 'Babble & Spin' the longest running and most popular regular column, bar none.

"Well, it was started by my maternal grandparents and EV's parents, who were big activists in the '60's. They were also trust fund babies, though I don't think they were terribly proud of it. Nor were their families particularly fond of the route they decided to take in life. I'm a little fuzzy on the details, but I believe EV's mother and my grandmother were roommates in college. My grandfather came from nothing, and everyone thought he married Nana for her money. Considering he was perfectly happy living off the land here, I guess they were wrong." Chloe paused, and Roger leaned in; he was thoroughly enjoying the story, so Chloe continued.

"Anyway, the two couples developed a strong friendship. They graduated college, and seemed to play the straight and narrow for a few years. As soon as their trust funds kicked in, they quit the corporate life and found this forest. A bunch of friends from their activist days heard about the project, and so they all teamed up to form a commune. It was all about living off the grid, exploring spirituality, and creating their own environment. Everyone worked together, pooled their resources, and shared everything." With a wink, Chloe reached over to spear a french fry off his plate. Roger blushed at the wink, but never noticed the theft of the fry.

"About 20 years ago, some of the first families left, including EV's folks. After that, local politics made it beneficial for us to become an official town. Members of the remaining first families formed an advisory panel that, over time, became known as the Board of Elders. They didn't want to deal with the hassle, so they proposed incorporation. EV had a meltdown; that's when she involved herself in town business. She knew it was our best move, and played a big part in convincing the rest of the commune to get on board. Taking charge like that turned her into the unofficial town matriarch."

Roger sat back in his seat and stroked his chin thoughtfully. "So there was never a snowball's chance in hell that you all were going to vote to merge with Gilmore?"

"Some of the younger residents were interested in *progress*, but no, on the whole it was a lock that we'd keep our own form of government. Our selectman system works for us; three people are elected each year, and so far nobody has gotten too big for their britches. The selectman's decisions are based on what's best for the *residents*, which naturally ends up making the most sense for the *town* as a whole. We're thriving—as far as we're concerned—and we don't need another town taking control."

"Well, there's someone out there who feels differently. The man who presented us with the merger proposal acted as though you'd all jump up and down at the opportunity of becoming part of Gilmore. And he acted like he was from the Pines, too." Roger seemed genuinely concerned, and Chloe knew she was close to getting a piece of useful information.

"Really? Maybe I know him. Who did he say he was? Do you have a name?"

"Oh, I have something even better." Roger pulled out his wallet and handed Chloe a business card.

Chloe turned the conversation to more mundane things, and by the time the dessert plates were cleared, Roger was fit to drive her home. He pulled into the driveway and turned off the car engine. "I had a great time tonight, and I'd really love to take you out again." Hope shined through bright as daylight when he turned to face Chloe.

"I did have a nice time, and you really are a great guy, but I'm interested in someone else, and don't want to lead you on. Do you think we could be friends? And I meant what I said about picking my brain. If there's anything I can help you with, please don't hesitate to ask." She bit her lip, hoping he would take the letdown with good humor.

"Well, it's disappointing, of course, but I appreciate your honesty, and it never hurts to have more friends. Good night, Chloe."

"Good night, Roger. And thank you, again." Chloe exited the vehicle and made her way inside. Closing the front door, she heaved a sigh of relief. It was never fun to hurt someone's feelings.

Chloe wandered into the kitchen, put a kettle on the stove, and dialed EV's number. "Tea, my place, ASAP." After changing into her comfy pajama pants and a tank top, and removing her makeup, Chloe returned to the kitchen. EV stepped in through the back porch door in time to hear the kettle begin to whistle. The path between Chloe and EV's backyards was getting a lot of use these days.

"So how was your date? Is Roger a stud muffin, or what?" EV teased, knowing full well that if Chloe was home by 9:30, the date had been a bust. Her plan was working out exactly as she had hoped it would. Now if Chloe could conquer her own fears, maybe she and Nate would finally come together. "I'm sure you saw the way Nate reacted to the idea."

Subtle, Chloe thought.

"Roger's nice actually; I felt like a huge jerk for leading him on. I let him down gently, and he took it like a man. *And,* he gave me something."

"What? Show me."

Chloe handed EV the business card Roger had offered.

"Nicholas Lane, Investment Banker. Works for the Barnard Group in Portland. You up for a road trip? I'll drive." EV would spare no energy ensuring that she didn't have to ride in Chloe's car; the words *death trap* perfectly described the battered Mini Cooper. The vehicle itself was fine, save for a few scratches and dents, but the driver was a menace to society. EV wondered how many tickets Chloe had racked up over the years.

"Okay, okay. You can drive. Let's plan for the day after tomorrow. First thing in the morning."

"My morning or your morning?" EV asked with a mischievous glint in her eye. Chloe responded with an eye roll.

"Put that rooster of yours out of my misery, and plan for a halfway reasonable hour. And bring coffee. Lots of coffee."

Chapter 3

EV was meddling in her love life. If Chloe hadn't been sure before, she was now.

How dare she? And seriously—hello Pot, my name is Kettle. Guess what? You're black!

Arms crossed, pouting lips set in mutinous lines, Chloe decided EV needed a taste of her own medicine.

Phase One—it was time to consult the one source she knew would have solid information about EV's past. Her foot tapped a beat against weathered ceramic tile as she leaned against the kitchen island and dialed Lila's number. Drumming fingers punctuated the tapping of her feet while she waited anxiously for her mother to answer the line. Lila could be anywhere in the world; last Chloe knew she was sunning herself on the Riviera, sipping cocktails served by hunky bronzed Frenchmen.

"Hello, darling." Lila's husky voice greeted her daughter.

"Hi, Mother, where are you now?" Sugar, one of Chloe's Siamese kittens, rubbed against her calf and curled a dainty tail around her ankle. She reached down to stroke Sugar's soft coat, scratching a favorite spot behind the kitten's ears and eliciting an erratic but enthusiastic purr.

"Tuscany, for the moment, but we're headed to Barcelona in two days. You could meet us, you know, dear." She sounded hopeful, but Chloe knew her mother didn't actually expect her to accept the invitation.

"I'm happy sticking close to home, but I hope you have a lovely time. Wait, who's we?" Chloe hoped her mother hadn't become embroiled in another relationship. Lila never had a hard time finding a man; in fact, she could have her pick. Willowy and blond, she was a taller version of Chloe. A healthy trust fund and a knack for investing negated the need for Lila to work a regular job; instead, she funneled considerable energy into maintaining her appearance and social standing. Well-known in certain European circles, Lila was considered quite a catch, and never lacked for male suitors. Foreign men flocked to her like bees to honey.

"Well, I *am* traveling with a companion at the moment. I haven't told you about Javier yet, have I?" Chloe rolled her eyes, but could practically feel the gleeful glow emanating from Lila through the telephone. Maybe this time would be different—but Chloe doubted it.

A leopard doesn't change its spots, Chloe mused while Lila waxed ecstatic about her new man.

Chloe *oohed* and *ahhed* in all the right places as she picked at her cuticles absentmindedly. It was time for a girls' beauty night, for sure. Mani-pedis, facials; the works. She'd call Veronica and Mindy later, and see what they were up to. Lila's excited voice brought Chloe back to the conversation briefly, but after a few more moments ticked by; she began to lose focus again. By the next time they spoke, she knew Lila would have moved on to her next conquest. So what was the point of absorbing information about yet another man she would never meet?

"I know you didn't call simply to check in. What's going on? Is everything alright?" Lila demanded after a long pause let her know Chloe wasn't really listening.

"Everything's fine, Mom, I just wanted to pick your brain about something."

"Go on." Lila sighed.

"What can you tell me about EV's past, romance-wise, I mean. Who was this guy who crushed her 20 years ago?"

Another pause while Lila considered.

"His name was Remy Vincent, and she thought he was her soul mate. The Vincents, along with your grandparents and EV's parents, were the first three families to settle on the commune. EV's father, Drew, studied agriculture, Remy's dad handled the engineering side of things, and your grandfather was a whiz with the carpentry."

"I remember Drew and Anna, but I'm drawing a blank on the Vincents."

"You didn't have much contact with them, and they passed away when you were little. Early on, Remy was all about the community spirit and, for years, the three of us were inseparable. I watched him start to crush on her. It happened so slowly, so softly, I'm not sure he even realized what was going on. Once he did, I watched him go after her until she fell for him, too. There was nothing soft or slow about it. She trusted him, and let him take her under."

"It's hard to picture her being that vulnerable."

"I honestly thought they would get the fairy tale ending." Something wistful ran through Lila's voice. "But as the years passed, I started to wonder if what I'd seen in him was love, or if it was simply the need to possess."

Chloe had hated him before she knew the details. Now that hate turned to loathing.

"EV has always been a force of nature. Looking back, I think he was more interested in taming her than wanting a true relationship with her. We were too young to know the difference at the time." What sounded like regret colored Lila's voice. "Once he started spending part of each summer with his grandparents, his attitude turned to crap; condescending toward EV; toward his parents; toward the way of life we all loved. EV made excuses, but I could see it hurt her. After a few weeks, he'd drop the attitude, and things would settle down a bit. I thought it would be okay in the end. They left for college together, and everyone expected them to come back and start a family, but it never happened."

"Was something wrong? Like, physically?" That

would explain why EV spent so much time among children, yet never had any of her own.

"I'm not sure. I was pretty tangled up in my own life by then. All I know is that they came back from college and, a week later, he was gone. You'll have to ask her if you want to know the rest."

"And what about you? Are you seeing anyone special?" Lila asked with mixed emotion. She wanted her daughter to have at least one meaningful relationship in her entire life, but not one that gave Chloe a reason to stay in Ponderosa Pines forever. Truthfully, Lila missed her daughter like crazy, but since they'd already fought about Chloe's decision to return home, she decided to stay mute on the subject.

"Actually, no. I'm not dating at the moment." Chloe's voice wavered slightly, which was a mistake. Lila was like a dog with a bone, and wouldn't give up until Chloe bared her soul.

"You don't sound so sure. I know you too well; I can tell there's someone you have your eye on. Spill."

"Well, I thought maybe Nate was going to..." Chloe trailed off; she hadn't really wanted to discuss Nate with her mother, but knew it was pointless to try and get anything romance-related past Lila. "But since the night Ashton tried to kill himself, he's been distant."

Lila breathed a sigh of relief. If Chloe had to get involved with someone in Ponderosa Pines, Nathaniel Harper would easily be Lila's first choice. She knew Nate. He was smart, honest, successful, and most importantly, wouldn't try to put her feisty daughter in a cage.

"My advice is: talk to him about it. Put yourself out there. What's the worst that could happen?"

I could embarrass myself; get rejected; ruin a life-long friendship. No big.

Bidding her mother safe travels, Chloe hung up the phone. Sugar's sister, Spice, joined the game of rubbing against Chloe's leg, occasionally swatting her sister away with the swipe of a paw.

Circling the kitchen island and breakfast bar, Chloe set out two dishes of wet cat food and watched the kittens fall on the treat like ravenous beasts. Good grief, they acted as if they hadn't eaten in a week. Once finished, they spent some time engaging in a bout of tandem whisker cleaning before following Chloe up the stairs to her home office.

Still annoyed with EV for setting her up on the blind date with Roger, Chloe's vindictive side reared its ugly head. She typed *online dating* into the search bar and surveyed her options. No, EV wasn't religious in the traditional sense, nor was she of Jewish descent; she wasn't a married woman looking to hook up with a married man; and Chloe hoped she wasn't into any kinky sex stuff.

Even the mere thought of that brought a shudder.

Deciding to take the traditional route, Chloe chose a service aimed at general matchmaking, hoping the site's promise to connect members based on mutual interests and dating preferences was legit.

Two hours later, she had completed an exhaustive survey to the best of her ability, and uploaded a photograph of EV taken at the beach last summer. Framed by the brim of a funky straw hat, EV, in partial profile, gazed out toward where waves crested foaming white peaks. Warm light from an impending sunset brought out the flecks of gold and bronze in eyes the color of good, strong whiskey that matched the sable hair tucked behind her ears. Even in repose, EV gave off a sense of vibrant motion. Chloe had no doubt her friend would soon be receiving a flurry of emails from prospective dates.

Hovering her mouse over the *save* button, she felt a momentary pang of guilt and nearly clicked *cancel* instead. Ignoring the feeling, Chloe remembered the look on EV's face after Dalton kissed her; with a little more of the story clear, she knew her friend was running from the past. Ultimately, Chloe hoped EV would get out of her own way, and make room for love—let Dalton into her life.

Maybe a few bad dates would make her realize exactly how rare it was to find a man like him. *Well, I can always take Mother up on her offer to travel if EV gets too pissed at me; Barcelona should be far enough away...*

It would have amused both Chloe and EV to know that their plans for each other were almost identical.

"...whole box of old rope. Right out of the shed—while we were in the house. We never heard a thing."

EV glanced over her shoulder to double check that it was, indeed, her own neighbor, Celia, speaking. More thefts meant more headaches for her, for Nate, and for Dalton; not to mention the mix of feelings she had over her town being invaded. Things had barely begun to settle after the last scandal. Another one so soon had her heaving a sigh filled with annoyance and anxiety.

Added to that, if this was the only mention she heard of the thefts all day, something was wrong.

Why had no one else put two and two together yet? This kind of thing usually burned its way through the grapevine with a vengeance—unless she had been cut out of the loop. But that would never happen, would it?

Still, harvest time—and autumn in general—was one of the busiest times of year for Ponderosa Pines. Battening down the hatches ahead of winter in the northeast took most people a few weeks.

For those who burned wood for fuel, there was the gathering, sawing, splitting, and stacking. Cleaning chimneys, tuning up snow-moving equipment, settling livestock, and putting gardens to bed for the winter had everyone scrambling to stay ahead of the first heavy snow, which could come anytime from mid-October on.

Feeding acorn squash into bushel boxes, EV figured this was probably the last of the year's fresh produce. Her own garden plot was barren now—save for the parsnips that would become sweeter when wintered over, and a patch of carrots in a sheltered spot that she was planning to cover with a generous amount of hay. Maybe that would be enough to keep the ground around them from freezing. Fresh carrots in the dead of winter would be welcome. And if the experiment went bust, she had canned plenty ahead.

The last box of squash was nearly full when Horis sidled up next to EV. If a man his size could sidle, that is. Tall and raw-boned, Horis sported his seventies-style Fu Manchu mustache with pride. He ran a hand through hair in need of a good barber, and pushed his bottle-bottom glasses closer to his eyes before whispering out of the side of his mouth, "Miz Baleston over at the school says a box of old art supplies has come up missing. She'd set them out on the back step and forgotten to bring them inside again. By the time she remembered to grab them, they were gone. It's an epidemic."

"She pointing fingers at anyone in particular?"

"Not so far."

"You have any thoughts on the matter?" Horis was a solid judge of character, whether that character was of the human or animal variety. Generally quiet, when he did speak it was with certainty.

"To tell you the truth, I don't see how it's any one of us from town. Don't make no sense at all. Everyone hereabouts knows they can ask for something they need or want. Most times people are happy to comply."

"Who would come in from Gilmore or Warren to lift a bunch of cast-offs and useless junk?"

Horis shook his head. "No sense at all."

Another thing to worry about—was the thought running through EV's head. On top of trying to track down a blackmailer with almost nothing to go on, now she was in for a bout of soothing ruffled feathers and placating raw nerves. Some days all she wanted to do was crawl back into bed.

Chapter 4

Much to EV's chagrin, Chloe was up and ready by eight o'clock in the morning, and she seemed less cranky than usual. The drive to Portland, which would have taken about an hour and a half in Chloe's car, took nearly twice as long in EV's ancient pickup truck. By the time the caffeine kicked in, Chloe and EV were fully enjoying the impromptu road trip.

"Skittle Pink!" Chloe shouted, pointing at a tiny fuchsia sports car racing up the other side of the road. "That's fifteen Skittles!"

"What on earth does a *Skittle* have to do with anything?" EV asked.

"Veronica's kids made up this game, and it's addictive. Pink cars are worth fifteen points; purple are worth ten; lime green are five; yellow and orange are three and one. The point system is somewhat arbitrary; supposedly based on how frequently each color is seen. Tractor-trailer trucks only count if the cab and trailer match. Oh, and if you see a cop car with the lights on, you can slap the roof and yell *Busted*! If that happens, you get everyone's points."

"Do you get extra points if the driver pees her pants when you slap the roof?"

Chloe gave her that look.

"I'm not sure I understand." EV said, "Where do the actual Skittles come in?"

"There are no actual Skittles involved; it's based on the colors of the candy."

"Well, that's disappointing. Skittles are my favorite."

"I'll buy you a bag at the next stop." Chloe promised. An hour later, EV was ahead by 25 Skittles, and Chloe decided a distraction was in order if she was going to make a comeback. "So, have you had any epiphanies about how this guy could be connected to the town?"

"The more I think about it, the less I feel like I know. The town, as a whole, is a close-knit group—we haven't had a deluge of new residents for quite a while. Based on Roger's account of things, our black-mailer spent some time in Gilmore schmoozing the board. I don't think he could live in the Pines and be able to pull that off without someone noticing. So that means—if this person is intimately familiar with our town—that he's either lived here or spent significant time here in the past. Skittle orange." EV pointed to a vehicle parked behind a tree up ahead. Chloe looked out her own window and rolled her eyes.

"I saw that. Anyway, there was a time when the Pines population was growing quickly. A lot of families came and went. That's when we built the school, and when Dalton opened his cafe. Some settled in, and others moved on. Yeah, there were some..." she paused to find a word that fit perfectly, "...dedicated types; we were a commune. Who knows what prompted this guy to come after us. At this point, I'm thinking he could be anyone. It's like a needle in a haystack the size of a skyscraper. I think all we can do is follow the trail and ferret him out."

"Yeah, you're probably right. Dedicated types? Is that a PC term for something else?"

EV grinned, but declined to answer. "Sabra came to town with a group of UFO..." again with the pause, "...enthusiasts. All of them believed they'd been taken for a ride at one time or another."

"I see. Well, that explains a lot."

"After that, we had a family of fruitarian nudists who were also practicing locovores."

"Who what-ists and what, now?"

"They ate nothing but locally-grown fruits and nuts. Unfortunately, half a winter of nothing but apples, frozen berries, and chestnuts drove them to look for a warmer climate where there were more options. They hadn't planned for it taking two years for most fruit trees to bear crops, so the variety was poor. And it gets pretty nippy in the winter, so that was a factor."

Chloe could listen to stories of the Pine's early days forever, and EV was happy to regale her with some of the more colorful tales.

By the time they arrived at the address listed for the Barnard Group, Chloe was in tears, and the game of Skittle forgotten. The street was quaint, but deserted. Small trees grew along the sidewalk, their roots buried in planting boxes every few feet; penned in by concrete on all sides. Never would they reach their full potential; their growth stunted in order to achieve an aesthetically pleasing height. Real estate signs posted in several office windows and the luster of fresh paint indicated that this part of town had undergone a recent makeover.

Hopefully, the office they were looking for was still in business.

"7998, that's it. We need suite 5." Chloe reached for the door, but EV continued driving, pulled into a space around the corner and finally shut off the engine.

"Why are we parking way over here?"

"Because Christine doesn't exactly scream *Hey, look. I have a boatload of money I'm looking to invest,* and we need a cover story if we're going to find out anything useful."

"Oh. Okay, so what's the plan? Am I your daughter, looking to ensure I inherit lots of cash?" Chloe teased.

EV shot her a disgusted look. "My niece will suffice, Ms. Smarty-Pants. Have I really aged poorly enough that I look like I might croak at any second?" EV tilted the rear-view mirror and studied her face for a moment. Aside a few thin laugh lines around her mouth and eyes, EV could have passed for at least 15 years younger than her actual age, and she knew it.

"Oh, stop, you know you've hooked me on your cold cream regimen—I've seen proof it works. Your face feels like a baby's ass. Now let's go."

EV searched the directory posted in the lobby for

the Barnard Group, and found them listed for suite 5, but when they reached the reception desk, it became clear that their cover wouldn't be necessary.

"We're looking for a Nicholas Lane. He left this business card with a friend, and we'd like some investment advice." Chloe pulled the card from her pocket and handed it to a frazzled-looking red-haired woman with an irritated expression on her face. "Barnard Group, can you hold please?" She barked into the telephone receiver, and hung up before the person on the other end had a chance to reply.

"There's no Nicholas Lane here, and that's not even one of our cards. I can make you an appointment with someone else, but it will be at least a week. We're swamped right now."

EV shot a look at Chloe and pushed for more information. "Is there any way for you to check and see if he's a former employee?"

"No need, I've worked here for several years, and I know all our employees personally. I've never heard of anyone by that name. Sorry." She returned to jockeying the unrelenting phone system. Chloe and EV trudged back to the truck in silence.

"Another dead end. This guy was smart, using a

legitimate business as a front. Now we're back to square one."

Chapter 5

Chloe followed EV's brown leather boots up the steps onto the hayride trailer attached to an ancient farm tractor, reached for the rail to hoist herself onto the platform, and promptly lost her footing. Uttering a strangled, "Oh!" and, bracing herself for impact, she closed her eyes tightly. Instead of hitting the ground with a resounding *thump*, Chloe felt strong arms beneath her and looked up, surprised, into the face of Nate Harper.

"Whoa, easy now. I've got you. Still clumsy as ever, I see." He grinned down at her, but didn't loosen his grip. It didn't escape Chloe's notice that he had one hand planted firmly against her backside.

Chloe scrambled to her feet and stood, facing him, willing her heart to return to its normal rhythm. *Adrenaline,* she thought, though she knew it hadn't kicked in until she realized who was cradling her in his arms. The last time she had seen him, he'd acted irritated and frosty. Now, apparently, he had gotten rid of whatever bee had been buzzing around in his bonnet. *Talk about mood swings.*

"Yeah, that's me, Clumsy Chloe." She laughed nervously and nearly tripped again, over nothing but a blade of grass this time. Taking her hand, Nate helped her onto the wagon, while EV watched the exchange with an amused expression on her face.

When the three had settled onto the bales of hay —Chloe squished between EV on one side, and Nate on the other—he finally let go of her hand with a gentle brush of his fingers. The sensation sent a shiver up Chloe's spine; she imagined him running his hands over other parts of her body, wondered what it would feel like to surrender to the nagging ache that had lately grown into a resounding throb.

Without warning, the wagon hit a bump, knocking Chloe out of her reverie, and nearly off her perch on the hay. "Someone said the Macs are really sweet this year, since it was such a warm summer. We should get some Granny Smiths too, so our pies aren't too syrupy." Chloe chattered nervously. "Applesauce would be good too. What kind of apples do you prefer for sauce?" This directed at EV, and accompanied by a desperate look that plainly said *help me!* EV pretended not to notice, but answered the question.

"A mix of several varieties—Ida Reds, Macs, Cortlands, and Braeburns. Gives a nice texture and body you don't get by using any one type."

Nate nodded as though he agreed, while EV bit her lip to suppress a smirk. Throwing Chloe under the bus, even if it was for her own good, meant jeopardizing the closest adult friendship she'd ever had. And yet, it was so tempting. These two were meant for each other. The only thing keeping them apart was total stupidity.

Two minutes of watching them play a round of sliding eyeballs—while neither one wanted the other to catch them looking—put a strain on her resolve. Not knocking their heads together put a strain on her resolve.

Not as big a strain as Chloe's constant shifting to create some distance from where Nate sat on the hay. Tired of being nudged and shoved, EV shifted to settle on a bale of hay across from them.

At the next stop on the hayride extravaganza, Veronica and her brood waited. Catching the younger woman's eye, EV gave her a subtle head nod to call

Veronica's attention to where Chloe now maintained a critical foot of space between herself and Nate. Quick to catch on, Veronica plopped down in the spot on Chloe's other side before directing her children to take up all the rest of the available space around them.

"Budge over, Chlo." Before Chloe had time to think of an alternative, her thigh was pressed tightly against Nate's on the one side, with Veronica giving no quarter on the other.

As always, nerves shot Chloe into a state of verbal incontinence.

"Look how pretty the leaves are right now. We should take some photos of the kids playing in them and get out the scrapbooking supplies." Chloe directed at Veronica, who merely nodded, busying herself unnecessarily with re-tying a tiny sneaker.

"The pumpkin crop is ridiculous this year." Chloe continued, nodding to a field full of bulbous orange gourds visible from their current view atop the crest of an apple tree-laden hill. "Even after all the decorating we did, there will still be plenty to carve in preparation for the Halloween Hike this year. Last year we lined the nature trail with, what, 250 jack-olanterns? This year we're shooting for at least 300. I can't wait."

The quirk on Nate's lips matched the twinkle in his eye as he listened to Chloe prattle on. EV could tell he found no hardship in cuddling up so close. A particularly nasty jolt as the tractor bounced through a rut in the path had him throwing an arm around Chloe—merely for stabilizing purposes, EV was sure —but when the ride settled out again, the arm remained.

When they reached the corn bin—the festival's answer to a ball pit for kids—Veronica stood to help her kids down from the wagon. The corn bin was a family favorite. Two feet deep, filled with dried corn kernels, it resembled a large sandbox. Or, as EV preferred to describe it—a litter box for kids.

"Bet you five bucks there's pee in that corn. You ever read about the things they find in those ball pit things? Thugs hide guns and knives in there. Kids lose dirty diapers." EV shuddered to think of it. "You let one of those forensic teams at it, and I'd bet you find all sorts of disgusting body fluids. Bacteria. You name it." She convulsed once more at the thought.

"Thanks a lot, Captain Killjoy," Veronica's expressive, cornflower blue eyes registered disgust. "Good thing I carry a container of wipes wherever I go."

Seeing her chance to escape, Chloe jumped down from the wagon, "I'll come along to help you keep an eye on things."

Her plan might have worked, except Chloe had forgotten Nate's addiction to apple fritters. The scent emanating from the nearby fritter booth curled around his nose and prompted him to hop off the wagon with a hungry glint in his eye. Luckily, Horis, who was currently in charge of the corn bin area gave her the perfect opportunity to break from the group when he called out, "Chloe, can I talk to you for a minute?"

"What's up?" She asked, gratefully, as she approached his post. Nothing much, as it turned out. The pair chatted about the upcoming holiday season, and the winter-preparation tasks were due for completion. Chloe relaxed and told Horis to sign her up for a couple of shifts. To Chloe's relief, by the time the conversation ended, Nate had wandered into the corn maze and disappeared.

Chapter 6

When the new email notification beeped on her phone, EV took the opportunity for a break in her leaf-raking duties, and glanced at the return address: *cutebobbie@funtime.com*. Spam filter fail—she'd deal with it later. Pocketing the phone again, she grabbed the water bottle she'd left on a stump, and glugged half the contents down in one go.

Two more chimes in rapid succession emanated from her pocket.

New email from *hoosyerdaddy648,* and one from *manlyman3*—both with the funtime.com address.

EV scanned through the emails. What she saw sent her into a slow burn complete with clenched teeth and a red face.

Someone had submitted her profile to an online dating site.

Chloe.

You're dead—EV texted Chloe after forwarding copies of the emails. She heard the soft bong that signaled an outgoing text followed by three new email beeps.

No wonder these idiots spent so much time searching for love online. If their emails reflected their personalities, at least half of them were horndogs.

Beep.

Prettyboy329? Did that mean there were 328 more of them? And the poor soul thought including a photo of him naked was the way to win her heart.

Beep.

Aww, this one sent a photo of his dog. No, wait. That was him from the back. EV turned off her phone. She seriously considered burning it. Or maybe having it exorcised.

This was absolutely the brattiest thing Chloe had ever done. EV gave her full marks for inventiveness.

But now? It was game on.

Cue the evil laugh, EV thought as she pulled out her phone to compose an email of her own. Carbon copied to four women she knew in Gilmore, and with a photo of Chloe attached, she wrote:

Remember that young woman I told you about? The

one who lives next door to me? I think she would perfect for your son. I could set something up he's interested. Get back to me ASAP.

Not ten minutes later, she had Chloe lined up for a date that very evening.

The doorbell sounded as Chloe was putting the finishing touches on her face: a light beauty balm foundation; a touch of mascara; and shiny lip gloss were all she typically wore. Tonight she had decided to experiment with a smoky eye. Kohl pencil shavings littered the bathroom vanity, and she had nearly smashed a bottle of liquid eyeliner in frustration; but the trouble was worth it. Her almond-colored eyes shone bright beneath thick, feathery lashes; the smudged liner and shadow blend coating her lids was subtle but sexy. *Good enough, especially since this date is a complete waste of time.* She had only acquiesced in order to placate EV. It had nothing to do with feeling guilty over the dozens of messages EV had received from a variety of randy older men. Nothing at all.

Taking a deep breath and preparing for the worst, Chloe opened the door to find a not-at-all bad-looking gentlemen holding a bouquet of flowers. "Hi, James. It's James, right?" She stuttered nervously.

"Yes, James Wright. Nice to meet you, Chloe." He practically salivated. His voice sounded feminine enough that she double-checked for his Adam's apple. He had one despite speaking in an obnoxiously high-pitched tone. *Ahh, there's the rub.*

"Let me put these in some water and we can go." Chloe tossed the flowers in an old ceramic watering can and bounced back to the foyer, herding James out the door before he got too comfortable. *And now he knows where I live. Fantastic.*

Gazing out to the driveway, Chloe noticed his monstrous Hummer blocked her car completely blocked from view, and she almost choked with the effort of biting down on an ecologically-minded rant. Chloe's Mini Cooper wasn't a hybrid vehicle, but it was still a heck of a lot more efficient than some giant beast of an SUV. And this guy didn't look like he was doing a lot of heavy lifting with it; the interior was pristine, and she could tell it was more status symbol than necessary choice. Nothing irritated her more than people who didn't care about the environment.

"I made a reservation at Delmonico's Steakhouse, if that's okay." James voice reminded Chloe of a whining child. Through gritted teeth, she managed a polite-sounding, "Sure."

Though she wasn't a strict vegetarian, Chloe made it a point to eat locally grown, grass-fed beef when she did imbibe, and Delmonico's was notorious for using the cheapest, most hormone-enhanced meat they could get their hands on. Didn't stop them from charging premium prices, though, and Chloe suspected James meant to impress her by throwing money around. Too bad that wasn't her style.

All she had to do during the short ride to the restaurant was nod and smile; James didn't notice she wasn't paying attention, what with his incessant babbling about the specs of his engine, and how much extra the tinted windows had cost. By the time they arrived, Chloe had decided she and EV were about even. Two hours later, she was sure of it.

"Veronica, help!" Chloe exclaimed into her cell phone. "I'm squatting in the bathroom, while my date inhales the *fourth* course of a dinner that will not end. I'm about to have a conniption. Please tell me one of your children has sustained a life-threatening injury and I must come right away? I'll give blood; a kidney even."

"They're all right as rain, but I can give you a call back in five minutes and pretend otherwise."

"Thanks, I owe you one."

"And I will collect. Love you!" Veronica's sign off was always the same, and even though Chloe knew it, the endearment always made her feel special. Veronica had a way of making everyone feel special. It was one of the things Chloe admired most about her. That and her willingness to partake in behavior Emily Post would consider questionable.

James looked crestfallen when, right on schedule, Chloe's phone rang and she insisted he take her home immediately. "I'm really sorry about this, but thank you so much for dinner."

He grudgingly complied, and Chloe flew out of the Hummer the second it came to a halt. "Thanks again!" she called, running inside and slamming the door.

Chloe realized she had grossly underestimated EV's penchant for revenge when two more random men contacted her, and she was harangued into going on dates with both of them. When they both ended up being complete whackadoos, Chloe's resolve kicked in.

For one, she intended to ferret out EV's ulterior motive—no one could contrive this brand of torture over nothing more than a few lousy emails.

Secondly, Chloe intended to throw EV under the

bus with Dalton the very next chance she got. Clearly, EV was processing something big, and needed a gentle nudge. Or a push off a cliff, if that's what it took for her to stop playing *Mystery Date* with Chloe's love life.

"You rotten old bat!" Chloe ranted into EV's answering machine when her friend failed to pick up the phone. "First I get to dine with a complete tool whose man bits must be itty-bitty to necessitate that monstrosity he picked me up in. I had to fake an emergency to get out of a fifth course at Delmonico's with that jerk. Then, a freaking Oompa Loompa shows up at my door with a bouquet of *my own* asters in his hand. He might as well have kicked my cat and peed on my doorstep! Then, to add insult to injury, I was forced to sit through *Final Destination 17,* or some such nonsense, and eat theater nachos for dinner!"

A resounding click let Chloe know that she had gone over the acceptable message length, so she called back to continue her rant.

"Oh, and date number three consisted of me huddled in the back of a pickup truck with a 12-pack of *Coors Light,* waiting for a meteor shower that isn't actually happening for another week, while a man who might have been considered attractive—save for the bushy back hair poking up through his shirt collar—tried to get me to go skinny dipping *in the freezing cold* on the first date! And by the way, you lunatic—get voicemail! Nobody uses an answering machine *with a tape* anymore! I know you're home, listening to this, you wimp! Your Christmas present is getting smaller and more irritating by the second! This is so not over!"

Chloe slammed the phone down emphatically, feeling a bit better after unloading her irritation on the responsible party. The only thing left to do was bake; it always calmed her nerves.

Chloe loved to both cook and bake, but each served a separate purpose. Cooking was easy: you could adjust the seasoning; throw something new into a recipe; or simply wing it and still wind up with something delicious, or at least edible.

Baking, however, required meticulous attention to detail. You needed the right ingredients, measured exactly; the correct type of pan or tin; and an accurate oven temperature. So, Chloe reserved baking for when she needed to either focus, or distract herself.

Setting the music app on her phone to the Colbie Callait channel, Chloe hummed along while measuring out equal parts egg, flour, butter, and sugar by weight. Two lemons worth of zest completed the sponge cake batter. After slipping the loaf into the 350-degree oven, Chloe juiced the lemons and mixed in some powdered sugar. She set the sticky glaze aside and danced around the kitchen island singing *Dream Life* until the cake was ready.

Chloe agreed with Colbie as she belted out the lyrics; she wanted to make her real life as much like her dream life as possible, and she had an inkling of what would make that wish come true. She also knew any judge from one of the umpteen singing competition shows now airing would describe her singing as *pitchy*, but she didn't care. Sugar and Spice seemed to agree and, after fixing her with twin looks of disdain, vacated the room. A blur of sleek, tawny fur, they raced up the stairs to snuggle up on *their* chair in Chloe's office.

A toothpick inserted into the center of the cake came out clean, so Chloe shut the oven off and used a skewer to poke several holes through the loaf. While still hot from the oven, the lemon glaze coated the top and dribbled through the holes, permeating the cake with sugary goodness.

Once cooled, it would set into a flaky crust.

Realizing she had nobody to share the tasty treat with, Chloe softened and shot a text to EV.

Lemon Drizzle Cake is cooling on my counter. Truce?

You overloaded my answering machine, and now must pay. I will accept cake as a peace offering.

Chloe smiled and made sure the back door was unlocked. All the thefts in town, despite their seemingly benign nature, had prompted Chloe to start locking her doors regularly; something she and nearly everyone in town had never felt compelled to do. Deep down, she knew her closest friend loved her to pieces, and that EV must think she had Chloe's best interests at heart. The pair couldn't stay mad at each other for long.

EV crept through the door and held up a small white flag. Chloe laughed, and any tension that may have been lingering immediately dissipated.

"So, you didn't like James, or Billy or Bob? Or was Billy Bob one person? I can't remember." EV smirked and received a pointed glare from Chloe.

"You're evil. And I want to know why. What bug crawled up your butt and made you decide to torture me?"

EV paused, choosing her words carefully. "Look, I know you're hesitant about getting into a relationship. And I know you have feelings for Nate that you're running away from."

This again, Chloe thought, while EV continued her explanation.

"I know I'm the queen of trust issues, but you don't have to join the court. I wanted you to realize that there are a lot of frogs out there. If you ask me, Nate's your prince. You both need to suck it up and be honest with each other. I thought you could use a gentle push."

"I'm not sure I'd use the word *gentle*." Chloe pouted. "And I know there's chemistry with Nate, but I also know that he hates it here. I finally found my happy place, and I don't have any intention of moving. He'll never settle down here, so what's the point? At least I can keep him as a friend this way."

"You don't even know what he's thinking. People change their minds. Would you rather kick yourself, or spend your life wondering?"

Chloe ignored the question, filing it away to think about later, when she was alone. "And what about you? I know you have more feelings for Dalton than you're letting on, and now that *you* know what else is out there, don't you think maybe he'd be the better choice?" Chloe pulled out her laptop and logged into EV's Funtime profile.

"*Partyboy69* sounds like a winner. He's wearing a Hawaiian shirt unbuttoned enough to show off a chest so furry, it looks like his beard went south for the winter. How do you feel about wall-to-wall carpeting? And would you look at all that bling. Even Mr. T would pity the fool." EV's eyes shot daggers at her friend as she settled onto a bar stool and started scrolling through prospective matches.

"A little bit of chest hair is okay, but if you've got to draw a line between neck and back hair, that's where I, well, draw the line. Oh, Jeebus, look at this one. *JaketheSnake* says the most personal thing about him is that he's a virgin. Wait, there's an update from last week that says 'Sorry, Ladies, not anymore!' I'm pretty sure I'm past the training stage, *thankyouverymuch*."

"That's just...the word *ew* isn't remotely descriptive enough." The next profile had them both laughing out loud.

"Isn't that Batman?"

"I can't tell. His beer belly is covering up the belt buckle. If it's not Batman, there's some weird S&M stuff going on. Pass."

"This one's actually kind of cute. *Niceguy57* likes Riesling, moonlit walks, and oh, never mind, wearing women's underpants."

"No cross-dressers please. I mean, no judgies, but not my scene."

"Ooh, *hungryforthebooty* is a *professional*," she made air quotes, "sign spinner in front of the Quiznos in Gilmore. I bet he could get you some free sandwiches if you showed him the junk in your trunk." Chloe's shoulders shook with laughter, and tears had begun to run down her cheeks as she struggled to get the words out.

EV did not grace her with a response, and instead kept scrolling. If she found something that actually made Chloe wet her pants, EV figured she deserved it.

"This guy looks like Santa Claus, and he's wearing one of those foam hats shaped like a block of cheese and holding a light saber. The caption reads, *Do you want your partner to be kinkier than you?* and his response is: *not possible!*" EV erupted into gales of laughter alongside Chloe.

EV popped open a bottle of Riesling in honor of *Niceguy57*, and the two settled onto Chloe's couch to continue crucifying all the prospective dates who shouldn't have ever been allowed access to the

Internet. By the end of the night, they had killed the bottle and laughed out any residual tension caused by their mock feud.

"I guess we're both better off meeting men the old-fashioned way. Though I might start doing a background check on potential dates, just to make sure they're not hiding a creeper profile in their web browser. Assuming I'll ever date again. Which isn't likely."

Chloe nodded in agreement. "That right there was enough to make me hesitant for a very long time. I think I need a shower!"

Chapter 7

Nate took a deep breath and glanced over at Dalton, who stood to his left. Noting the marginally less nervous look on Dalton's face than his own, Nate willed his body to settle down. An 8-foot-high, ornately carved set of double doors loomed in front of them; on the other side sat a conference-style chamber reserved for the town elders' use. Nate had visited the room only one other time, and had felt the same level of anticipation then as he did now. He knew it was ridiculous; he saw these people out and about town on a regular basis, and had known them all for his entire life. Yet, somehow, all of them grouped together made Nate feel like a teenager who had gotten into trouble, and now must explain his behavior.

With the Selectman system in place, there was no need for a secondary governing body, which made the town elders something of an enigma. Technically, they had no legislative function or role in the everyday decision-making processes—that fell to the elected officials. Few of the newest town members, and even some of the ones who had lived there longer, had any idea why the town had elders, and why they had the last word on certain decisions.

Nate was hazy on the details himself, though as he understood it, the Selectmen saw to it that Ponderosa Pines met all the rules, restrictions, and fiscal responsibilities required by the state in order to maintain their status as a town. The elders, on the other hand, held sway over those issues that were specific to the founding tenets around which the town was formed. Between them, EV and the elders were the heart and soul of Ponderosa Pines—its conscience.

It was to that conscience Nate hoped to appeal.

The doors opened and the two men were ushered in and offered seats at a large rectangular table already occupied by the six town elders. Marjorie Hillard, Johnathan Lewellyn, and Dalton's parents, Edward and Elizabeth Burnsoll occupied one side; Nate and Dalton sat across from them, bookended by Louise Naughton and Martin Craig.

Marjorie was by far the most outspoken with

Martin Craig's demeanor directly opposing her own. He was the oldest—and most revered—elder, and tended to stay quiet until interjection was absolutely necessary. When he did speak, everyone listened. Johnathan Lewellyn, whose wife Priscilla owned the local yarn shop and hosted a regular knitting group, had been active in town business for years before his recent appointment to the board.

"So what brings you two in today? Must be serious to have requested a meeting with all of us." Marjorie asked. Dalton's parents kept quiet, but smiled encouragingly at Nate's pinched expression.

"We would like to discuss the blackmail letters that were written to Evan Plunkett, and the possibility that this person could continue to target the town. He approached Gilmore's town officials and convinced them that we, as a town, wanted to merge with them. Obviously, he stood to gain something big, or why would he go through that much trouble? And he used an alias, which is that much more damning. What if he tries again? We, Dalton and I, are requesting your support in continuing the investigation, with the intent of exposing the blackmailer and ensuring that he doesn't continue trying to undermine our town." Nate made his initial plea with genuine concern showing on his face.

What little evidence Nate had found was nowhere near enough to keep the investigation open, except as a civil matter.

The other five elders turned toward Martin expectantly, and he answered gently, "The proposal was shot down; it's never going to happen. We don't want to merge with Gilmore. Nobody can force us to disband the town, and when it comes down to it, the Pines is stronger at its core. I don't think we're in any danger at this point, and we have no evidence that this man has done anything illegal."

"Why go out looking for trouble where there is none? If something else comes down the pike, we will certainly address it. But I think we should conserve our resources for the time being." Johnathan chimed.

"What if this person is dangerous? I know he didn't actually kill Evan, but he did threaten to expose him. Who knows how far he would have gone. What if he decides to target someone else? What if he targets the town again, with more ammunition this time? Are we doing our civic duty by letting this go? I don't think so." It was the first time

Dalton had spoken up, and he looked to his family for support. It was his father who responded.

"We appreciate your enthusiasm, both of you." Edward cleared his throat and nodded at each of them in turn. "But the matter is closed. We are in no danger, so why waste resources in trying to catch someone who isn't a threat. Thank you for your time, gentleman."

"But…" Nate began to protest.

"The matter is closed, Nathaniel." Elizabeth's cool voice put an end to any further argument, and Nate and Dalton were bid farewell and escorted to the door. "Don't worry, you two. Everything will be all right."

"Well, that was a colossal waste of time. Did you get the impression they had already discussed the situation and made a decision before we even opened our mouths?" Nate asked with frustration after he and Dalton had returned to their tiny shared office.

"I've never had much luck arguing with my mother; I didn't expect today would be any different. My parents are descending into old age, and their level of urgency has certainly declined. I admire their confidence, and maybe they're right. But I don't think so."

"So we keep pushing? On the down-low?"

Dalton paused for a moment, weighing the options. On the one hand, they could be searching for a needle in a haystack; or the needle could in fact be a match, one that would set the haystack ablaze and take Ponderosa Pines down with it. "We move forward with the investigation, however we can."

"I know someone who might be able to help. Elise owes me a favor—a big one, so she'll handle this for us on the down low. I'll make the call first thing in the morning."

"And if we find nothing, nobody, will be the wiser. Including my parents. If we're right, and we can take this guy down, they'll have no choice but to eat their words."

Chapter 8

Arriving home after enjoying steaming mug of cappuccino and a plate of biscotti at the Mudbucket—and a chilly walk through the woods—Chloe opened her front door and immediately knew something wasn't right. No pitter-patter of little paws bounding up to climb her pants like a tree; Sugar and Spice usually greeted her at the door, but tonight, all was suspiciously quiet.

Chloe flipped the wall switch, illuminating the entryway, and crept stealthily around the corner into the living room. Something dark and winged floated from the far end of the room. In the split second it took her to turn and race back the way she had come in, Chloe recognized the intruder as a bat. Safe outside, she slammed the door behind her. Leaning against the wall for a moment to give her pounding heart a chance to slow, she fumbled around in her pocket, dragged out her cell phone. Barely stopping to think, she dialed Nate's number.

"There's a bat in my living room! The kittens are in there, and I didn't see them when I opened the door. Help!" Chloe blurted as soon as he answered, ignoring the way her heart leapt at the sound of his smooth *hello*.

"And I'm the only person you could think to call?"

"Just get over here, please!" she shouted before hanging up.

Pacing back and forth outside the front door 15 minutes later, Chloe nearly burst out laughing as Nate jogged up the driveway dressed for bat battle. Glove-covered hands brandished an old butterfly net; jeans tucked into work boots, and a hoodie pulled tight around his face completed the ensemble.

"Okay, where is the little sucker?" he asked, tapping the net against his free hand while attempting a menacing expression that was diminished by the obvious fear in his eyes. Nobody liked dealing with a possibly rabies-infected bat. Chloe covered her mouth with her hand to mask a smirk; she pointed toward the door, eliciting a grumpy look from Nate as he squared his shoulders before propping open the screen door. "Living room," came her muffled response.

"Get in your car and wait for me." He commanded. She did as she was told. Nate braced himself, then raced inside. Chloe heard some banging followed by a loud expletive. A minute or two later, a black shadow swooped out through the open door and into the night. Still worried about her precious babies, Chloe leapt from the car to run into the house.

"Nate? Where are you? Sugar and Spice?"

"They're fine, Chlo, I found them." Nate called from somewhere upstairs. She followed the sound of him cooing to the kittens, it lead her into her bedroom where Nate crouched on the floor. One hand holding up the dust ruffle, he leaned over to peer under the bed while he talked baby talk to the kittens in an attempt to coax them from their sanctuary. He stood up and moved aside slightly, forcing her to brush against him on her way by. Not taking his eyes off her, Nate stepped back and peeled the hoodie away from the tight white t-shirt he was wearing underneath. As he pulled it over his head, revealing a set of exquisite abs, Chloe nearly lost it.

"It's pointless," she said quickly. "They won't

come out from under there until they're ready. Come downstairs, I'll make you a drink while we wait." She had to get Nate out of her bedroom before the idea of what the "V" of his chiseled obliques was pointing toward caused her to jump him, right there on her rumpled bed. Turning away before any more naughty thoughts occurred to her; Chloe led Nate back to the kitchen.

"I see half a bottle of coconut rum, some melon liqueur, and bubble gum flavored vodka." Chloe declared, after searching her cupboards for cocktail fixings.

Nate shot her a bemused look. "From what, Barbie's after-Prom dream party?"

"Ha ha; you're so funny. It was girls' night. No judgies." Nate couldn't help but notice the way Chloe's shapely hips flexed as she stood on tiptoes to check another cabinet. He bit his lip and tried to hide the fact he'd been staring at her ass as she whipped around holding a half-full bottle of bourbon. "Ah-ha. I knew I had *something* manly in here."

Two hours later, and several sheets to the wind, Chloe sat cross-legged on the kitchen island, gesticulating wildly while relaying a story from her last trip to London

"...so my Mother, in her infinite wisdom, decides we'll simply camp outside their hotel and wait for them to come out. All this trouble, and when they do come out, Robert Smith isn't even with the rest of the band. Her obsession with The Cure has always confused me, but it wasn't until that moment that I realized how deep it ran. Not for nothing, but we ended up spending the rest of the night singing karaoke songs at some random pub. You should have seen her belting out "Mint Car." It was hilarious. I do miss her."

She trailed off, becoming suddenly aware that Nate was staring at her with desire in his eyes. The look on his face matched hers from earlier, when she had been dangerously close to giving in to an errant impulse. Fortunately, the kittens chose that exact moment to make their reappearance.

Spice made a beeline for the food dish, apparently having come close to starvation during her stay under the bed. Sugar, however, launched herself onto Nate's lap. Tiny claws dug through denim and into flesh, emitting a startled *yelp* and an irritated grimace that softened into a smile when Sugar let out a loud *purr* and rubbed her head against his chin.

"You're lucky you're cute, little one." Nate chastised gently. *And he's a cat person.* Chloe thought to herself. *But that's irrelevant*—she tried to dismiss the notion.

"Want me to walk you home?" Chloe asked, not sure what answer she was looking for.

"Sure, as long as you're not afraid to walk back by yourself." She poked her tongue out at him and swatted him on the arm. It took a single comment to turn him from *sexy man* Nate into *childish boy* Nate.

Crisp autumn air prompted Chloe to cross her arms and pull her sweatshirt close; Nate slung a casual arm around her shoulders and they fell into a comfortable silence until, trying to sound no more than mildly interested, he asked, "So what's up with all the dates I hear you've been going on lately? Any keepers?"

Chloe allowed the question to sink in for a moment before responding. "No, not likely. EV decided to stick her nose in my business. First it was Roger, that guy from Gilmore." She looked at Nate out of the corner of her eye to gauge his reaction, but his face was blank. "Though that was more a fact-finding mission, anyway. She wanted me to see if he could tell me anything about the man who proposi-tioned Gilmore to merge with Ponderosa Pines. It didn't pan out, by the way. The business listed on his card has never heard of him. Nicholas Lane probably isn't even his real name."

"You didn't need to go out with Roger to find that out. I got his name and checked out the investment company as soon as we realized he was playing both ends against the middle. I'd bet money it's not the only alias he used, and I'm looking into it. It's police work now, Chloe. You and EV may know everything that's going on around here, and I know you can do some serious Internet research, but in order to track this guy you'd need the skills of a first-class hacker or a private investigator."

His voice was stern, a warning for her not to get involved again. She wondered if he cared more that she was butting into his investigation, or that she could get hurt in the process. They were silent for a few more moments before Nate continued prodding.

"So that explains *Roger*, but what about the others?"

"Well, after she set me up with him, I wanted revenge, so I set EV up with an online dating profile, and when she found out she vowed to get even. Now I've been propositioned by every weirdo in the area." She caught herself before adding,

What EV really wants is to convince me that I need to date you.

"Well, I'm sure you'll find a way to politely disentangle yourself; and lob the proverbial ball back into her court while you're at it." He kept his tone light to hide his relief. He was still annoyed, but knew he couldn't stay mad at her forever. As they approached Nate's front stoop, he pulled her close to him under the guise of a friendly hug, closed his eyes, and inhaled her perfume.

Chloe's head spun as she breathed him in; a combination of body wash and deodorant mingled with his natural musk to create a scent that was uniquely *Nate.* She looked up into his face, longing for him to kiss her and realized, for the second time that night, she was in trouble.

No, Nate thought as he nearly gave in to the temptation to taste her full bottom lip before realizing they were both still a bit tipsy. *If it's going to happen, I want us both to have a clear head when it does.*

As he pulled away, Chloe's face fell. She tried to hide her disappointment, mistaking his reluctance for disinterest. *Well, I guess that's that. Maybe the whole thing is too weird for him. EV doesn't know what she's talking about.*

Nate stepped inside, closed the door, and leaned on it for support. Never in his life had it been so difficult to practice self-control. He turned, opened the door again, and nearly called out to Chloe before he realized she was halfway up the block, hoofing it back to her house. He couldn't see the pained expression on her face, or the tears that wet her cheeks. Her name stuck in his throat, and by the time he could make a sound, she was gone.

Chapter 9

"You know, Dalton, I thought when I moved back here it would be easy as pie; I certainly didn't realize that I'd be dealing with murderers, blackmailers, and thieves. It was never like this growing up. I hope it's nothing more than a fluke; can't imagine a crime ring breaking out in Ponderosa Pines." He smiled wryly.

"I think we're safe. These thefts are getting blown way out of proportion. But we need to get the busy-bodies off our back. If they get there before we do, we'll never live it down."

"With all this ruckus going on, I haven't had a second to even check my messages. Let's see if any of the stones we've managed to turn over were hiding our favorite neighborhood blackmailer." Nate pulled out his cell phone and hit the voicemail and speaker-phone buttons, expecting nothing but police-related business.

After all, his social life was fairly non-existent, and the one person who consistently called him was currently sitting at a desk to his right. Nate wasn't prepared for the cloying voice of his mother, and quickly switched off the speaker when he heard her distinctive *Hello*.

Dalton stifled a laugh when Nate's fingers weren't fast enough to keep him from hearing her refer to him as *Pooks*, a childhood nickname Nate despised, but couldn't seem to convince her to stop using. Cheeks flaming, Nate decided to listen to his messages privately, in case anyone else had decided to leave him a humiliating voicemail.

Barbara Harper, his dear mother, was one of the best prosecuting attorneys in Portland. Her opponents might think of her as a shark, but she turned into a fluffy bunny when it came to her only son. He had grown to accept her overbearing nature as compensation for making her career a priority, and leaving most of the childrearing up to Nate's father, Martin. The two were used to being on their own together; Nate had stayed in the Pines after the divorce, while Barbara moved to the city and buried herself in her work.

She'd been thrilled when he took a job at the Portland Police Department, and had inserted herself firmly into all aspects of his life. Now that he and his Dad were living under the same roof again, she had gone back to her distant ways. Nate wasn't complaining; her attention had begun to feel oppressive, and he didn't have the heart to tell her to back off. Martin Harper's attitude was much more *live and let live*.

Getting some distance from her was another check mark in the plus column for relocating back to the Pines for good.

Bingo, the next message was from a police detective in Gilmore, with whom Nate had attended the academy.

"Harper, it's Grady. Found a couple of trustworthy citizens to work with a sketch artist on your phony investment banker. Didn't turn up any legitimate leads in facial recognition. I'll email the sketches to you, but I think your hunch is right; this guy's white collar. He has used a couple of other aliases, so maybe you'll get somewhere with those. That's about all I can do under the radar. Let me know how it goes."

Nate made note of the three aliases Grady

provided. "Well, Deputy, we've found a little something. Let's see if we can turn it into a lot."

"He's not a ghost, so he's gotta be out there somewhere. If anyone can find out where he's laying low, it's you."

Chapter 10

Dalton was the first person to see a figure in the woods, though, by the time he had gotten home from his evening hike, he'd convinced himself the twilight was playing havoc with his eyes, and what he'd seen was a deer. Before long, more reports of curious sightings began to trickle in.

The Winslow boys, aged eight and ten, swore they'd seen the boogieman watching them through the trees one night when, instead of sleeping, they were looking out the window for their dad to come home from installing a set of his hand-built cabinets for a family down in Warren.

A few days later, Nate received a call from Tank.

"Harper. I don't know if this is anything or not, but last night—I guess it was around eight—I heard a commotion out in the barn. Something spooked the horses. By the time I put my boots on, and made it out there, they were settling down, but I think I saw a bear going into the trees."

"You sure it was a bear?"

Tank paused to think about it. "Now you mention it, I guess it could have been a man. If it was, he moved like a bear—sort of hunched over, with a limp." Tank paused again. "Or a lurch."

"You want me to come out and take a look around?"

"Nah, nothing to see. Checked this morning; didn't find a thing. Just thought you should know."

Small town detectives, Nate thought, *ought to leave the investigating to the pros.*

"You'll call me if you see anything else?"

"You've got my word on it."

A day later, Fleet Van Eck staggered into The Mudbucket and swore he'd seen a hellhound with blazing red eyes. Since Fleet's own eyes were red, glassy, and his breath could knock over a tree, no one placed a lot of stock in his account.

Night fell like velvet around where Sabra Pruitt— wrapped in a blanket, and clutching the remote shutter release for her digital camera—sat in her back yard. In the two hours since midnight—spent huddled in a folding camp chair—she'd already counted thirty-two meteors.

The tripod-mounted camera, fitted with a fish-eye lens, sat an arm's length away, its glass eye pointed straight up in order to catch the most night sky possible. The soft click of the shutter was almost inaudible among the occasional call of a night bird, and the trilling of cicadas. It was so peaceful; she struggled against falling into a light doze, while hoping to capture multiple light tracks as the shower kicked into high gear.

When the first rustling noise reached her ears, she figured it for a 'possum. Maybe a raccoon—certainly nothing larger than that and refocused her attention to watching for streaks of light among the field of stars blanketing the sky. She'd no sooner caught a rare multiple streak as four separate meteors flashed overhead, when she realized the rustling noises sounded closer. Louder.

Curiosity, rather than fear, drove her to lean over; to reach for the twist handle that would flip the camera back to its upright position, so when the mysterious figure came into view she was ready to hit the button on the remote. Assuming she was about to get a night shot of a deer, Sabra waited patiently and without fear. The flare gun on the table next to her might not be the wisest thing to shoot into the woods, but it would turn away a coyote or a bear. Probably.

Hours spent in moonlight had sharpened her vision enough to see the dark shape moving through the woods. Not a coyote; it stood on two feet. A bear? Breath coming quickly and her heart pounding a staccato beat, Sabra had to concentrate to move without making noise as she reached for the flare gun, cradled it in her lap—just in case. Daddy always said not to provoke a bear. If she sat quietly, it would probably pass on by. Sabra pulled the blanket higher, covered all but her face in its fluffy darkness, and watched until the figure broke from the cover of the woods.

It was close and coming closer.

It didn't move like a bear, but it didn't look like man, either.

Out of reflex, she punched the camera remote. The shutter slid open and closed. The quiet click seemed loud to her ears but the sound didn't carry past the edge of her patio.

Deliberately furtive, the man-thing sneaked toward the apple trees, where the last of the season's blow-downs lay in a litter on the ground. Sabra glimpsed a head of shaggy hair, but the hand that reached out to pick through the pile looked human. In a short time, several apples disappeared into what she thought was a pack or bag of some kind, before the shaggy head turned toward the house.

Definitely not a bear.

Shadows fell over the face so Sabra couldn't make out features, much less any facial expression.

Barely breathing, she watched the intruder move toward the open-sided lean-to addition attached to the side of her small barn. A muted clatter slid across the air. Sabra imagined those white hands picking through the contents. What he might find useful, she hardly knew. Most of the detritus were items she had picked up at various flea markets—things she planned to *do something* with at some point in the future.

Most of her finds ended up as part of a series of aborted art projects that never saw the light of day —or even worse—did. Several she gave as gifts to some of her friends. Priscilla Lewellyn had been the befuddled recipient of Sabra's most ambitious project to date. The severed head of an antique carousel horse that Sabra had repainted and mounted for hanging. It might actually have made an interesting piece if not for the fact Sabra had spruced it up using a set of glitter paints intended for Christmas projects. Now the red, gold, and green horse head with its bared teeth and flashing eyes—red, glittery ones—hunkered above the toilet in Priscilla Lewellyn's tiny guest bathroom, looking like some demented hunting trophy from a North Pole massacre.

The Yeti—for that was what Sabra had decided she was seeing—emerged from her storage area carrying an old metal grate she'd picked up because it had a floral pattern worked into the wrought iron. Indignant that she was being robbed, but not stupid enough to call attention to herself, she snapped a couple more photos as the figure lumbered off into the night, carrying its prize.

When only the hooting of an owl broke the relative silence, Sabra deemed it safe to gather her things and move back inside. Meteors still shooting past went ignored, forgotten in her haste to get safely behind locked doors.

Her heart still beat a strong tattoo against her chest. Excitement was already edging out fear, now that the feeling of being invaded had lessened, and her imagination had already begun generating scenarios—each one more fanciful than the next.

Sabra's boon companion, an impossibly fat pug dog named Muggly Puggington, followed her to the bedroom to watch with adoring eyes while Sabra changed into a pair of soft, bright red fleece pajamas printed with snowmen and penguins. While he waited for her to get into bed so he could snuggle up, a stray strand of doggy drool dangled toward the floor. Each raspy inhale sucked the drool back up like a sloppy little yo-yo.

As with every other room in the inn, Sabra had painted her bedroom in a warm, earthy tone. In this case, brick red. A collection of empty perfume bottles ranged across the dresser like shining jewels. Though Sabra might not be able to manage more than simple craft projects, she had a knack for choosing exactly the right pieces to compliment her decor. A matching metal grate to the one the Yeti swiped from her cache sat on the chunky, dark-stained fireplace mantel recycled from an old support beam. Below the mantel, lay the hearth—another project up-cycled from its previous life—a grinding wheel from an old gristmill.

It was too much work to start a fire, so Sabra

decided to snuggle under the covers, where she tossed and turned for the next half hour. Too keyed up to read or to sleep, she finally threw back the covers, and gave in to the inevitable. The camera lay where she had left it—on the kitchen table next to her laptop, which she now opened and turned on. While the computer booted up, Sabra scrolled through the images in the camera's small view screen before impatiently flicking the power switch. She pulled out the memory card and shoved it into the laptop's onboard reader.

Seconds later, a slide show popped onto her screen. An hour before, the streaks painted with light across a velvet sky would have enchanted her, but that had been BY. Before Yeti.

Now all she could think about was whether she'd captured the elusive being in pixels. Forty or so impatient flicks later, she came to the first image. Trees, grass, and deep shadows were all that she could see, even when she was looking at the exact spot where he had stood. She scrolled again, then once more, and stopped.

There. By the apple tree, she made out the hint of his outline and the small patch of lighter color where she had seen his reaching hand. He'd been moving too fast against the already dark background to get a good shot.

Scroll.

Scroll.

And there it was. The money shot. He'd paused long enough in one place for the camera to capture a distinct impression of him against the side of the barn. The shaggy outline of a man-thing.

Sabra clapped her hands in delight and shared the photo on Facebook with a single word caption.

Bigfoot.

By the time Sabra—thankful for once that the Inn was unoccupied—dragged herself out of bed, her Yeti photo had already been shared thirteen times. In the hour it took to post the meteor shots to her profile, her blog, and all her favorite forums—shares of the figure hit seventeen. She replied to some of the comments on the image before flipping the laptop closed.

Sabra paced around the kitchen twice in a haze of indecision. What she should do—in fact—what she should have done last night, was call Nate Harper and Dalton Burnsoll, and tell them what she had seen.

And be branded a total fruit loop.

Granted, it would be a level up from her current status as a partial nut case, but that wasn't the kind of status she wanted to increase. Someone needed to know, though. So she did the next best thing. She called EV.

"Can you come over? Right away?"

"Is something wrong?" Sabra sounded breathless with some emotion. EV couldn't tell if it was excitement or fear.

"Please come as soon as you can." Telling would make it more real. Sabra hoped EV would hurry.

Ride or run? Biking along the main roads or running through one of her woodland shortcuts would take EV roughly the same time to get to the Come On Inn. So, naturally, EV decided to try biking through the shortcut to save time, and managed to shave minutes off the trip without whacking her head on any low-hanging branches.

When Muggly Puggington pulled his usual attack-the-bike caper, she spared him a quick word before knocking on Sabra's heavy front door, which flew open mid-rap.

"Get in here," Sabra glanced in both directions to make sure EV was alone.

What was up with all the intrigue?

"He was here. Last night. He stole a piece of metal grating from my collection."

"Who?"

"The Yeti."

EV's mouth dropped open.

"The what? What did you just say?"

"Yeti. You know, Sasquatch." When EV still stared uncomprehendingly, Sabra elaborated. "Bigfoot."

"Have you been brewing your own beer again? Eating funny mushrooms? I don't even think those are all the same thing. I know none of them exist."

"Cute. Real cute. I have pictures to prove it. Come on, I'll show you."

Sabra flipped open the laptop, waking it up from hibernation. The slide show was still open and cued up to the best shot of the figure by the barn.

EV leaned down for a closer look. It was a man. There was no such thing as a Yeti. But she had to admit, it did look damning. In silhouette, the figure looked shaggy from head to toe. Not a bear—the shapes were wrong.

"Can you send me a copy of this? And don't show it to anyone else until I've had a chance to check it out?"

Sabra dropped her eyes before turning back to the computer.

"I'll email it to you right now." She did so with a series of clicks. "But I already posted it on my Facebook page."

EV blew out a breath. Of course she had. Because that's the first thing people did these days. Slap every little thing up on social media for the world to see.

"Can you take it down?"

"It's too late. The image has already been shared," Sabra looked at the updated numbers, "twenty times now."

Another gusting sigh escaped EV's lips. "Well, tell me how it happened." She slid into a chair, and listened to Sabra tell the whole story.

Halfway home, EV stopped her bike. Caught between laughter and tears, in the end, she managed both. Somewhere in between, she sent off a text to Chloe.

Totally bizarre experience, tell you when I see you. Be prepared for shock and awe.

Chapter 11

Veronica and Mindy in tow, Chloe pushed through the front double doors of Mama Nancy's diner. A dull roar of conversation met her ears, the tinkling of silverware against porcelain punctuating the din. The scent of greasy fried food recalled the last time Chloe had eaten here; Nate had taken her out for a night of people watching and binge eating. Comparing the experience to the several questionable dates she had been on lately, Chloe had to admit there was a layer of sexual tension with Nate that, so far, remained unmatched. More than that, though, they laughed at the same things. Under the sexual tension was something deeper; closer. Something that added layers over and around the chemistry. It scared her to death.

Please seat yourself read the sign in front of the hostess station. The three made a beeline for an empty prime corner booth. What Chloe saw across the restaurant made her stop in her tracks; Mindy plowed into her backside, emitting a startled, "What the..." before noticing Nate sitting at a table across the room. With a woman. A beautiful redheaded woman Chloe didn't recognize. Pulse racing, she could feel the blood rise to her cheeks as pure jealousy and anger bubbled up inside her.

"Turn around!" Chloe hissed at her friends, but it was too late.

Pasting a fake smile on her face, Chloe approached their table.

Thank goodness there's no thought bubble above my head.

Thought bubble or no, Nate knew Chloe well enough to realize she wasn't happy. The concept made his own heart race, while a hopeful feeling rose in his chest; maybe she really did have feelings for him after all. Plus, it served her right for going on all those dates. He didn't care if EV *had* set them up: she could have said no, or at least given him a heads-up.

"Hi, Chloe. This is Elise. Elise, my *friend* Chloe." If Elise noticed the emphasis on *friend*, or the tight expression on Chloe's face, she didn't show it.

"Nice to meet you." She said, flashing Chloe a genuine smile.

Bitch. And a nice bitch too. Those are the worst.

"Nice to meet you, too. See you around, *Nathaniel.*" Chloe spun on her heel and stalked back toward her friends, who were watching avidly from the booth they had snagged. Nate nodded to them, and they both waved half-heartedly, unsure whether to act friendly or pierce him with a patented *you-hurt-my-BFF-and-now-I'm-going-to-kill-you* look.

Chloe, plunking herself down facing away from Nate, began peeling the paper napkin away from a bundle of silverware, one layer at a time. Veronica and Mindy gave her a full minute of silence before pouncing.

"Okay, what was that all about? Last time I checked, you couldn't care less who Nate was seeing. I thought he was *just a friend.*" Veronica blurted out, casting a knowing look at Mindy.

"I thought so too, but it seemed like maybe he wanted more. Then it seemed like I wanted more. When he came over to help me with the bat, I thought he was going to kiss me, but..." Chloe was lost in thought, and Mindy took the opportunity to interject.

"What bat? Details please."

"A few days back, I walked through my front door

and there it was. A freaking bat in my living room—just swooping around." Chloe shivered. "I called Nate, and he came over to get rid of it."

"Okay, and? How did you go from shooing away bats to nearly kissing?"

"Well, I made us a couple of drinks and we... talked...for a while." Chloe's cheeks burned pink at the memory of Nate's exposed stomach. "When I walked him home, he hugged me, and it seemed like he wanted to kiss me. But he didn't."

"Want us to take him out for you? I know a good place where we can hide the body." Veronica offered with mock-seriousness.

"We could take him out and let the Yeti have him." Mindy supplied.

Chloe softened slightly. "Let's give him another chance before we resort to ritual sacrifice. Speaking of which, can we please take a minute to talk about this whole Sasquatch business? Could things get any weirder around here?"

Neither of her friends bought the change in conversation; they'd comply for the moment, but more details would be required before the night was over.

"No kidding, we've got our very own Bigfoot. He's

definitely the one who keeps stealing stuff from town. It's odd, though, the things that have been disappearing. Mr. Zellner is pissed," she stretched the word out long, "about his pornographic scarecrow." Veronica snorted at the thought.

"Why, was it anatomically correct? Because that would be stranger than someone stealing his clothes!" The three erupted into giggles; Chloe tossed her hair and shot a glance in the direction of Nate's table. His eyes slid back to his now-empty dinner plate without meeting hers, but Chloe suspected he had been watching her since she sat down. Like his scent, she could feel the weight of his gaze, even when she wasn't looking directly at him.

"I've been meaning to ask you, why on earth was there a giant Hummer in your driveway the other night?" Mindy brought the subject back around to Chloe's love life. She had run into EV Torrence at the Mudbucket earlier, and already knew EV's plan for uniting Chloe and Nate. It was one that she and Veronica were happy to perpetuate, for the sake of their friend's sanity and happiness.

"I've been rented out like a common streetwalker, that's why." Chloe couldn't hide the sarcasm dripping from her lips. "You two are lucky; you have no idea what it's like out there. *Sex and the City* sure got it wrong. There's no bevy of sexy, eligible men; not even if all I wanted was a fling. And believe me; I'd get flung right about now if I thought it would take the edge off. Problem is—that's not what I really want."

"So why don't you try talking to him about it?" Veronica asked gently.

"Because if Nate wanted me, he'd let me know. He wouldn't have pulled away, and he wouldn't be lunching with gorgeous women, and flaunting it right in front of me. Besides, the end result won't be pretty. His shoulder is nearly healed; he'll be heading back to Portland soon, and I've had enough long-distance relationships to know they never work out."

"Portland is only an hour and a half away. He's not moving to Siberia. I think this whole deal is a cover because you're scared. Yeah, you could lose a friend, but you could also gain a partner. And you don't know what he's thinking. He might surprise you."

"I'll think about it." It was the same statement she had made to EV, but so far, all thinking had gotten her was a muddled brain and a feeling of para-lyzing self-doubt. "But for now, let's move on to happier subjects. I don't want to look like I'm agonizing over here."

"Did you see Eliza Blackburn's baby girl? Speaking of Sasquatch...I know people think all babies are cute, but she looks like one of those goblins from *Labrynth*."

When Dalton promised something, he delivered. It was one of the things EV liked best about him. He pulled her into Drifters where the DJ was spinning exactly what she had requested—pulse-pounding rock.

Of the vintage variety.

Warm fingers curled around hers; Dalton led her toward a table in the back, where there was at least a snowball's chance in hell they could hear each other if they wanted to talk.

"You know this stuff is actually oldies," she pointed out when something from the early years of Kiss started to play. "That's probably why the crowd is fairly tame. Can't have us seniors in a mosh pit. No room for our walkers."

Dalton grabbed her hand. "There's nothing senior about you, or the way you make me feel. I could swear I'm fifteen again."

"I remember you at fifteen. You were quieter than

you are now. A little awkward. A little shy. Good sense of humor, though. And you always helped the smaller kids." She gave him a warm smile. "You haven't changed."

"Is that a good thing or a bad thing?"

"A good thing."

"I remember you at fifteen." Dalton chose his words carefully. "All knees and elbows. Long hair flying when you ran; and you were always in a hurry. Always running." He ran his thumb over the back of her hand in a gentle caress that sent an electric shock down to her toes. "Are you still?"

"Hmmm?" She'd gotten lost in the sensation.

"Are you still running?"

Deliberately obtuse, she answered, "Three days a week. Keeps me in shape."

"You know what I meant."

"Let's dance." *And change the subject*, she thought, as she pulled him onto the small dance floor.

It was answer enough. He followed her willingly.

EV's plan—at the time—had been to choose dancing music that would force him to keep his distance. Given the option of a do-over, she might have made a different choice. The idea of being with Dalton was growing on her. Like a fungus.

Until he started to dance.

His moves looked like Elaine from *Seinfeld* and Carlton from *Fresh Prince* had a baby. Needing to see if people were staring, EV added a full turn. When she spun back to face him again, he was cracking up.

"Gotcha," he mouthed before moving into a smooth rhythm that matched her own.

She flashed him a grin. The song ended, and the next one began with a strong beat. EV let herself fall into the music until it took over her body, giving her time to think.

How long, she asked herself, *has it been since you've done anything more than date and dash? Since you felt comfortable enough to laugh with someone?*

The way Dalton's eyes rested on her felt like a balm laid over her soul. The empathy he showed in that single look said he wanted her in more ways than merely the physical. Not since Remy had she let a man get this close to touching that vulnerable part of her where *need* lived.

But do you want him? Could you love him?

God help her, the answer was yes.

Chapter 12

Deciding to funnel her frustration into productivity, Chloe settled into her second-floor home office and booted up her computer. Her column had been all over the place the last few weeks; she covered the deaths that had occurred, along with the aftermath. Ponderosa Pines had been turned upside down after the loss of the Plunkett brothers, and Chloe had tried to use her column as reassurance that everything would be alright.

Now, things around the Pines had mostly returned to normal. Though she wasn't grasping at straws for material, it was back to the usual small-town gossip that was her bread and butter.

Chloe checked the *Pine Cone* automated tip line and received a deluge of comments regarding the mysterious figure seen traipsing through the woods, along with a number of what could only be described as complaints about disappearing items. She transcribed the details of each tip in a notebook, the way she always did before opening the *Cone*'s Facebook page. That's when she realized her town was in for a rough ride.

Sabra's post had gone viral. In two day's time, her Yeti photo garnered 96 shares. Sasquatch enthusiasts from around the country were positively giddy at the possibility of a real, live Bigfoot. Chloe clicked on Sabra's profile and read through each comment.

The vast majority of responses were of the logical variety; many people seemed to think the photo was touched up, while others claimed to see nothing more than a hairy man. Still, it was the believers, no matter how small a subset, that made Chloe nervous.

She clicked on a few twitter hash tags left by the more exuberant comment posters, and discovered a couple of groups dedicated to the investigation of seemingly-legitimate Sasquatch sightings. Not only had Sabra created a buzz, she had also given away her exact location via the inn's Facebook page. Now any weirdo who actually thought the photo would lead to an authentic Bigfoot sighting could click a link and download directions to Ponderosa Pines.

Chloe had no choice but to cover all legitimate

news—and this was surely legitimate news— but she hated to add more fuel to the fire. Setting her concerns aside, Chloe penned the latest edition of 'Babble & Spin' for the *Pine Cone*.

> *Hey, Piniacs, are you ready to dish? Looks like things around the forest haven't completely returned to normal. A certain inn owner caught a photo of our Midnight Marauder taking some building materials back to his hideout in the woods. Sure, he looked a little like a Sasquatch, but let's be real, people! Internet notoriety for mystical creatures probably isn't the best way for our town to stay under the radar.*
>
> *And what's this I hear about our favorite police officer being spotted at Mama Nancy's with an attractive redhead? Sorry, Ladies, but it looks like Inspector Hottie might be off the market after all. I thought for sure he'd wind up with a well-known blond on his arm, but perhaps I was mistaken...had to happen sometime, right?*
>
> *Speaking of which, how many dates can one gal go on over the course of a week?*

Blondie has been spotted leaving her house in a different vehicle several times—and returning home early each evening. Maybe she'll find a pearl among the oysters, but for now, it looks like a bust.

Last, but not least, remember that Yetis are sneaky. Local law enforcement needs all the help they can get—so let 'em know if anything else goes missing. Ta-ta for now!

Chloe hated writing about herself more than anything, but figured she could at least use her column to get a rise out of Nate. Besides, the occasional tidbit kept people from suspecting her as the anonymous author. If her identity were revealed, she'd probably lose her position at the paper—not to mention the dubious distinction of being first 'Babble & Spin' columnist in history to be outed. That was not an option, so she proofed and printed the copy without another thought.

"I want my ceramic gargoyle back." Lottie Calabrese ranted to EV, who had rushed over to Lottie's after receiving a panicked, incoherent phone call. "Engelbert belongs in the middle of that patch of mums." Lottie explained, pointing a wrinkled finger.

"He was there yesterday afternoon when I was raking leaves, and late last night when I let Drambuie out. Now he's gone! Kidnapped! It's that thief the police can't seem to catch; I know it!" EV couldn't help wanting to chuckle at the urgency in Lottie's voice. She was assuming Drambuie was the cat, and Engelbert was the gargoyle.

Lottie owned Open House, one of two almost-identical establishments located on the same road—the infamous Sabra was her neighbor and business rival. Mostly, Lottie hoped to land a husband; which was why she took on long-term lodgers and gave preference to any good-looking male applicants. Today, even in her hysterical state, Lottie had taken the time to apply a full face of makeup and hoist her considerable breasts into a push-up bra that truly did seem to defy gravity.

Looking over Lottie's shoulder at a car in the distance, EV asked, "Did you call Nate Harper about this?" An answer was unnecessary; Nate rounded the corner at the end of the street, ramrod posture showing determination; he headed straight for Lottie's driveway. EV's hawk eyes registered the change of expression that came over his face when he caught sight of her: irritation mixed with grudging acceptance.

Ignoring EV, save for a polite nod in her direction, Nate spent a few minutes listening to Lottie describe the scintillating events of the previous evening and this morning. Once he had taken down the information, and collected a photograph of Engelbert—without commenting on the fact that Lottie actually *had* a photograph of a ceramic gargoyle—Nate slid back into his car. Before he could put it in gear, EV hopped into the passenger seat. "Can we talk for a minute, please?" she asked in a sweet, but unconvincing tone.

"Cut to the chase, EV. What were you even doing here? You live farther away than I do, so she must have called you first. Now, I realize that *kidnapped* ceramic gargoyles aren't the most exciting cases, but they're the most exciting we're going to get in this town, and it would be nice to at least be the first call in the event of an.. um... emergency." Nate finished lamely.

"She did call me first, and I'm sorry that's an affront to your considerable manhood, but it's beside the point. I know you don't appreciate my input, but this whole Midnight Marauder business has me a little worried. You know that photo Sabra posted has gone viral, don't you?" Nate nodded. "And there's a group of people who think it's the real thing—Bigfoot hunters, for crying out loud. Sabra's profile includes the inn's address; I wouldn't be surprised if some of them showed up here."

Nate's right eyebrow, which had been slowly rising during EV's proclamation, had now hit its limit near his hairline. "You're telling me you think a bunch of Bigfoot hunters are going to show up in town looking for proof of an authentic sighting?" He ran his hands through his hair in a characteristic gesture, causing it to spike up in all directions.

"That's exactly what I'm saying. If we can figure out who this guy actually is, maybe we can take the heat off the town. And stop this theft nonsense, which would definitely get things back to normal around here. I'm getting a little tired of intrigue, to tell you the truth."

"Hold on a second. First of all, there is no "we" here, unless you mean myself and Dalton. You are not a detective, and you need to stay out of this so you don't get yourself into trouble. I've already started researching missing persons and similar crimes. This person could be dangerous, no matter how innocent these thefts may seem." Nate warned with a pointed frown, though he knew it wouldn't be the last time he would have to have this conversation.

"Okay. Okay, I give. I'll try to stay out of it; but I can't guarantee my neighbors will let me." Even though she knew it was childish, EV crossed her fingers behind her back. She did not intend to stay out of it—no matter what—still, she would play along if it would get Nate—and Dalton—off her back.

"So," she said, changing the subject abruptly. "What's going on with you and Chloe?"

Nate trying his best not to look taken aback, affected a stony expression, and answered. "You know I've always thought of you as a second mother, but you do know I already have one meddling, pain-in-the-butt, don't you? I really don't need another one. What's going on between Chloe and me is between the two of us. I think you've done enough, setting her up on all those dates."

And there it was; he wouldn't have mentioned the dates if he wasn't irritated by them. Her plan was working. It might not look like it now; in fact, from the outside, EV was sure it would seem that Nate and Chloe, as a couple, were doomed. However, her vast experience told her that this was the eye of the storm; all would come to rights in the end.

"Point taken, Nathaniel." She patted him on the hand that was still resting against the gear shifter and exited the car with a wry smile. *Yes, I think it will work out, after all. Maybe I should give them one of those cute couple names like Noe or Chlate. Or maybe not.*

Chapter 13

"Thanks, Elise; you have no idea how much help you've been. My hands are tied here; I really appreciate it."

"Don't even mention it, Nathaniel. You've pulled me out of so many jams; I'll still owe you even after we find out who this scumbag is. Remember when you wrestled that cheating husband off me after he caught me taking photos of him with the barely overage stripper? What's more, I like your little town. It's so homey and, well, a little quirky, but in a good way." Elise looked around *The Mudbucket,* where she and Nate sat at a corner table near the kitchen door.

She was thoroughly enjoying the Chai latte Rhonda had dropped off, along with a tray of blintzes that looked like white sugar sin and melted in her mouth. "I wonder if I could get Deanna to come check this place out; I bet she'd love to take some photos at one of those festivals you've told me about.

Bottom line, these people don't deserve this kind of harassment from some jackass with ulterior motives."

Nate tried to ignore the gnawing feeling in the pit of his stomach—the one that flared up protectively whenever he thought of someone trying to screw with his hometown. As much as he hated to admit it, he was getting more attached to the place every day. He'd left as a callow youth thinking this place was too small to hold him. Or, if he was being brutally honest, that it held too many memories of his mother. Now, that the feeling of home was creeping back, he couldn't stand the idea that someone would try and ruin what his family had helped build.

"How is Deanna? I haven't seen her since that dinner party at your place. I still dream about her yeast rolls, by the way. If you wanted to repay me, maybe we could work out some kind of installment plan with baked goods." Elise laughed out loud at the dreamy look that swept across Nate's face.

This was one man whose heart connected straight to his stomach. And the jerk certainly didn't look like he ate his weight in carbs on a daily basis, but she knew that fact was true.

"I'm sure she'd be happy to accommodate that

request. As far as she's concerned, you're up on a pedestal. I don't know how you manage to turn every woman in a ten-mile radius into butter, including those of us who could care less about your man parts."

"Must be my magnetic personality." He intoned wryly, revealing uncharacteristic self-doubt. Elise pounced on it, quick as a cat.

"What's up? Did you find someone immune to your charms?" She asked, remembering the beautiful blond woman Nate had introduced to her during their last meeting.

Nate ran his fingers through his hair in frustration. "That was Chloe. And she is, apparently, immune to me completely. It was stupid of me to think she would ever see me as more than her small town friend. No woman has ever held a candle to her, in my opinion. You know what my dating history consists of: it's not exactly stellar, to say the least. I thought this was my shot, but maybe it's time for me to really move on."

"Are you blind, or just stupid?" Nate's head whipped up to face Elise straight on. Emotion flashed in his eyes and he gave her a questioning look. "Women who aren't interested in a man don't go all

PMS the second they see him having dinner with another female. You didn't feel the ice when she saw you with me? Trust me, I know women—in more ways than one, I might add, and I know when a woman has the hots for someone. My friend, Chloe is totally into you."

"Then why does she keep pulling away? It doesn't make any sense." Nate looked miserable as he picked at his chocolate eclair.

"Have you talked to her about it?"

Nate shifted uncomfortably in his seat. "Not exactly."

"Well, what's holding you back?"

"She's been jet-setting her whole life. She's been everywhere; seen everything. And I've been here—well, not here," he gestured to indicate the town, "but here-adjacent, plugging away at my career. How can I believe she'd actually be happy settling down with me? At any moment, she could decide she misses her nomadic existence, and run away. Then what would I do?" He finished, miserably.

"How long has she been in town this time?"

"Three years."

"Seems like wanderlust would have kicked in by now if that's what was going to happen. And, I thought *you* had no desire to stay in this town. Aren't you planning on heading back to the city to reclaim your detective post once your shoulder will allow it?" Elise fixed him with a pointed stare. "Maybe she thinks you're going to take off, and leave her alone here."

It was a shot in the dark, but Elise had no idea how close to the truth she had come. However, it was the first time Nate had thought about the situation from that point of view.

"I guess that's a possibility. The thing is—I've been having second thoughts about going back to Portland. My apartment has sat empty for months, and I don't even miss it. The city never felt like *home*, not the way my Dad's house here does. I pay out the ass for utilities; someone else takes care of the maintenance; and I'm left with zero sense of accomplishment.

Getting back to my roots has made me realize that's not how I was raised, and it's not what I really want in the grand scheme of things. I thought I'd get married, move to a suburb somewhere, and at least have a home and a life. Instead, I eat greasy takeout every night, and my fridge is full of beer and condiments." He waved his coffee cup at her. "I don't even mind living with my father for the time being. It's given us a chance to spend some quality time together. Communal living is starting to look more appealing by the second." *Especially if I'd be communally living in Chloe LaRue's vicinity.* He added silently.

"Sounds like you have a bit to talk to her about. Don't shut her out, or assume she knows what's running through your head. Or that you know what's going through hers."

"You sure you like this private investigator gig? You should have been a therapist. Can we get off the topic of my love life?" He'd had enough of that for now. "Tell me, what did you find out about that alias? Have you come across a real name yet?"

"That's why I wanted to see you. It's looking like there's more than one person involved in this whole scheme. I've found several bits of information, and some of the records overlap. It looks like he's in two different places at once, which is impossible. Alias #1 checked into a hotel in L.A. at the same time alias #2 was shopping in France. He—or they—have been careful to stay away from security cameras, at least in the States, and I'm not getting anywhere overseas. I did get one hit on a lead that seems connected to someone who used to live here. Does the name Remy Vincent mean anything to you?"

That name was familiar to him. Nate knew he'd heard it recently, but now he couldn't remember in what context. "I'll look into it."

He tossed some cash on the table, nodded toward Rhonda, and followed Elise outside.

"Thanks, Elise. Bring Deanna over for dinner sometime soon. I'll cook." Nate hugged his friend before depositing her into her car and watching her drive away. He had a lot to consider; maybe it was time he came clean and told Chloe how he really felt. But first, he'd get the skinny on Remy Vincent.

"We got something!" Nate burst into the Deputy's office, where Dalton sat behind his desk eating a foot-long turkey Panini from the Mudbucket. A side salad sat untouched, his eyes having been much bigger than his stomach. Dalton pushed the sandwich aside and looked at Nate with rapt attention.

"Does the name Remy Vincent mean anything to you? It's the one name that Elise could find with any history. It's not an alias." Dalton's face flushed; his blood ran hot as storm clouds formed behind his eyes. He stood to begin pacing as best he could in the confined room. Anger radiated off him in waves.

"Yeah, I know him. And if he's involved, you can bet he won't stop until he's destroyed the Pines."

"Okay, what's the deal? What does he have against the town? And why do you hate him so much?"

Dalton sighed. "He's EV's ex-fiancé. I honestly don't know what she ever saw in him. He put on a good front; played the dutiful citizen, but it was all surface. The jerk had EV convinced he was the patron saint of Ponderosa Pines while he was chasing her around, though. She fell for it. I couldn't blame her; really, he put on a convincing act."

"Give me all the details, no *Reader's Digest* version, please. The whole scoop."

"Here, eat the other half of my sandwich and I'll tell you the whole story. But some of it's personal, and I'd appreciate if it stayed between the two of us." Dalton handed Nate the untouched half of his Panini. Talking about Remy Vincent was enough to make him lose his appetite.

"Of course." Nate settled into his chair, took the sandwich, and nodded his agreement.

"Remy Vincent is the son of one of the founding members of the commune. You've seen the photographs hanging in the town office, right? Check them again and you'll see the Vincents right next to the Torrences and the LaRues. Anyway, growing up with Remy you could tell he thought he was Ponderosa Pines royalty, as if that were even a thing." Dalton rolled his eyes at the memory.

"I've lived here all my life, so I had a front row seat for the whole show. He was sneaky, and he knew when to hold his cards close. The commune was in a period of steady growth back then." Dalton remembered aloud, "It was a tight-knit core of true believers, you could say. Quite a few early members had realized the amount of work involved in building and maintaining the property; for others it was a phase, and once it passed, they moved on. Anyone still here more than 15 years later was *committed*. Contempt for our way of life wasn't really tolerated, so Remy toed the line and kept his opinions mostly to himself."

Fists clenched at his sides, sneering, Dalton added, "He was pretty vocal about them as long as EV wasn't around, though. Whether he cared for her or not, he was determined to have her. She was beautiful and vibrant; even as a teenager. Full of vim and vigor. He put on an act good enough to make everyone think he was in love with her; maybe he was, I don't know. I never thought so, though. What I do know is that whenever she was around, he played the part of a dedicated environmentalist, activist, and any other *ist* he thought would appeal to her sensibilities."

"And you had a thing for EV, too, didn't you?" Nate nodded as though he already knew the answer.

"Yes, I did. I thought the sun rose and set on her. Still do. At the time, I was awkward and full of self-doubt. I didn't stand a chance. Whenever Remy left during the summers, EV and I spent a lot of time together. As friends, of course. She was loyal, and she waited for him." Admiration and frustration colored his words.

"Every year, he'd come back with a chip on his shoulder. He had spent enough time around his snooty grandparents to further inflate his already sizable ego." Frustration ebbing away, Dalton sank back down in his chair; rested his elbows on the desk.

"For short periods of time, Remy showed his true face. He treated EV like she wasn't good enough for him; made pointed comments about how provincial we all were. But Emmalina wasn't a woman a man easily turned away from; he knew enough not to let her go, whatever his motive might be. They worked it out, and eventually, I washed my hands of the whole situation. I figured if she still couldn't see him for what he was, there wasn't anything I was going to say to change her mind. Marlene moved to town, so I turned my attention to someone actually attainable. By the time EV and Remy returned from college, we were happily married."

Nearly finished with his story, Dalton shrugged.

"Remy didn't stick around, and before he left he shot his mouth off to anyone and everyone about how much he despised this place. Marlene and I were in the process of setting up the cafe when he strode down Main Street and had a temper tantrum in the middle of the square. Yelling and carrying on about how backward we all were, and how much he hated this place. Nearly broke his poor mother's heart. She wouldn't even mention his name for the longest time. I think his folks were the only people in town who weren't relieved to see him go."

Nate looked puzzled. "Where are the Vincents now? I know they don't live here anymore..."

"Well, a couple of years after Remy took off; they

were headed to a conference about solar energy solutions at MIT. They missed their commercial flight, and someone from the conference offered them a seat on a small private plane. The plane left Portland, but never made it to Boston. Both of them died, and evidently, Remy had their remains shipped back to wherever his grandparents were located. He never even came back to clean out their house; he laid that responsibility on EV's mother and father. It wasn't too long before Drew and Anna Torrence returned to mainstream life. I think there were too many ghosts here for their liking."

"Sad story. How have I never heard about all this? People in this town gossip with absolutely no shame about the smallest of things, and this goes in the vault?"

"Yeah, the pendulum swings both ways. When someone is truly hurting, the residents of this town can lock a story up more tightly than Fort Knox. It's one of my favorite things about the Pines: we're all family, and we protect each other."

"Yes, it's one of my favorite things, also." Nate stroked his chin thoughtfully. "So he has no ties here, and he hasn't been back for years. What kind of vendetta could he have against the town?" It's been decades since he left, and he has shown he's willing to go to some length to try and screw us over." Dalton caught the possessive term. He hoped his job would still be safe if Nate decided to stay. He pulled his attention back to Nate, who was still speaking, "We need to figure out what's in it for him. Seems like he'd have moved on a long time ago."

"I guess we have work to do, boss. And let's keep the girls out of it this time; there's no need for EV to know that a blast from her past could be lurking around. I'm not letting this asshole take her away from me a second time." Dalton's mouth set in a hard line, and Nate realized how deeply the situation with EV had cut him—after all, he could relate.

Nate sympathized with Dalton—in a manly way, of course. Affection bubbled to the surface, the deputy was growing on him; Nate knew they'd make excellent partners and great friends. If they got the chance—but he wasn't making any long-term decisions right now. At least one more piece of the puzzle needed to fall into place first.

"I agree completely. Besides, at this point he doesn't know we're on to him. I've had a hunch this whole time that he has an accomplice in town. Let's not tip our hand; we'll keep quiet about what we know until we're sure who we can trust. I'll get Elise to cross-reference Remy with everyone in town. If he's still connected to someone here, she'll be able to tell us who."

Chapter 14

On the third glorious day of an unseasonably warm snap of October weather, EV stepped out of New Sage—Ponderosa Pine's answer to the we-carry-everything big-box store. From the front, New Sage looked much like every other shop lining the short block that passed for downtown in Ponderosa Pines.

A few years back, a transient artist offered to ply his trade by cladding the entire block of storefronts using decoratively cut cedar shingles. The elders had been happy to let him stay in a vacant cabin. He'd spent the entire summer doing three things: painting the view from the top of Hogarth Ridge; installing what amounted to a cedar shingle mural spanning both sides of the street; and trying to talk EV into bed with him.

By the end of the summer, he'd succeeded at all three.

When it was time for him to leave, he did his level best to persuade her to go with him, but nothing he had to offer was enough to pull her from the Pines. He'd driven away leaving her with exactly what she had wanted from him—fond memories, and nothing more.

That had been the way of it with her, and no matter what Dalton Burnsoll wanted, that was the way it would stay.

Liar. Her inner voice all but shrieked it.

Speaking of the devil or merely thinking of him must have been enough to pull Dalton from wherever he'd been lurking, because no sooner had she finished the previous thought, than he'd turned the corner and was headed her way.

"Treat you to a coffee, Emmalina?" his eyes roved, with appreciation, over the well-worn jeans and flannel shirt she wore. He used her given name deliberately, just to see her expression.

"Sure, Earnest. I'll take a coffee, Earnest." Two could play the name game.

Too bad they had both crapped out in the name department. He hated Earnest Dalton almost as much as EV despised Emmalina Valentina. Then again, when she said his name, it didn't sound so bad.

The grin was still on his face when he set a cup of coffee in front of her, following it up with the plate of maple-glazed donuts he'd hidden behind his back. He was just opening his mouth to speak when they heard a low rumbling.

"Sounds like a prop plane." Dalton searched the sky.

"Not a plane." EV watched the road leading into town. "Something else." *Something that's going to make my life hell*, she thought with a sense of impending doom. Sometimes, no matter how strong and capable they might be, her shoulders ached from the weight of the status she carried in this town.

"Probably just passing through, no worries." Dalton hoped he was right.

"Not with my luck lately."

The first vehicle came into sight.

Vintage was the kindest word EV could think of to describe the motorhome lumbering toward her. *Total heap of rusty junk,* were the words closest to the truth. Old, and in a state of disrepair, evidenced by the cloud of exhaust it belched into the air. For all the noise it made, the vehicle moved exceedingly slowly.

Keep going. Just do not stop here, please. EV silently urged whoever was driving the behemoth vehicle. Alas, she was doomed to disappointment. The camper pulled to stop right in front of them, which gave EV and Dalton a chance to observe the images painted all over it.

What they saw was some sort of woodland scenes featuring a group of hairy-looking men. She was just trying to wrap her head around that when Dalton nudged her arm and pointed. Two panel vans and another, smaller, similarly decorated camper pulled up behind the first. Antennas bristled from the roofs of all four vehicles.

EV glanced back at Dalton to see his habitual grin was gone—replaced by a mouth set in grim lines.

What had him riveted? A sign emblazoned across the larger of the two vans: Sasq-Watchers. Underneath in smaller print, Yeti: He's Out There.

"Dalton, do you carry a gun?"

He lifted an eyebrow at her.

Of course, he did. He was a deputy.

"Well give it to me."

"EV, you can't shoot them just because they're delusional."

"Not them." EV gestured toward the caravan of fools. "I'm going to go kill Sabra Pruitt for posting that picture on the Internet." Her words were measured; her voice dry as powder. "I knew I should have made a bet with young Nathaniel when I told him this might happen."

His grin was back.

"Maybe they won't stay." he repeated.

"Yeah? Well, maybe a pig will fly out of my..." The sound of a motor home window sliding open cut off her derision.

"Excuse me, ma'am. Can you tell me how to find the Come On Inn? I mean...this *is* Ponderosa Pines, right? I'm looking for Sabra Pruitt." The polite voice came from a scruffy man of indeterminate age.

EV flashed Dalton a sardonic, I-told-you-so look before beginning to provide detailed directions for the Inn until Dalton cut her off.

"We were just heading out that way; you follow us, and we'll take you right to her."

"Thank you, sir. That's much appreciated." The face withdrew.

"Come on; EV. Let's take them to their leader. It'll give us a chance to see what's what."

Once in the car, she grumbled, "You can laugh now, but I'd put money on this not ending well. And don't even think about telling me how you and Nate will take care of things, because no matter what happens in this town, it ends up—somehow—with trouble knocking on my front door."

Dalton detected a note of bitterness.

"I thought you loved being the go-to person in town."

"Have you ever noticed me accepting a job in town office? I'm all for helping my neighbor, no—my extended family—because that's what this town is to me. But there's a system in place that could work more efficiently if people used it more often. You're part of that system, and you get left out of the loop all the time."

"You should know, since you're one of the key players in the *screw the loop* game." It was Dalton's turn to sound bitter. "Do you have any idea how I felt when Ashton Worth had you at gunpoint? You should have called me when you figured out it was him."

"Well, since I didn't know for sure until I found him in my house, that would have been difficult."

Defensiveness turned her sullen. "I would have called you once I was sure." It might have been true. She was almost sure it was.

He pulled up in front of Sabra's place and sniffed the air. "Do you smell smoke?"

EV didn't smell anything, "No."

"Well, you should, since it's your pants on fire." He narrowed his eyes when she tried to hide a smirk. "This discussion isn't over," Dalton promised. "Come on, let's go see what Sabra's gotten us into now."

She followed him to where the motor home was disgorging its passengers.

The man who had asked for directions was the first to step out. Ignoring Dalton and EV, who watched with horrified interest, the man reached back through the door where someone they couldn't yet see handed him enormous video camera, complete with a microphone on a boom. Deftly, the man strapped himself into the apparatus while an entourage formed around him, using strips of duct tape to secure some of the dicey-looking straps.

"Sweet Jeebus, it's Larry, Daryl, and his other brother Daryl." EV whispered.

Dalton tried to stop the laugh that burst into his

throat, but all he managed to do was turn it into a snort. "Not quite, look how fast they're moving," he pointed out.

In just a couple of minutes, the group had assembled into a complete camera crew. EV wished she had a chair and some popcorn when, as one, they approached Sabra's front door. She didn't even feel bad about letting Sabra face the music on her own. The innkeeper had started this circus; she might as well ride the elephant.

The guy EV thought of as Larry, the ringleader of this motley group, rapped his knuckles hard on the dark-stained wood. He glanced back over his shoulder to check that his crew was in place. Once a long moment had passed, he turned toward EV with a questioning look. She gave him a small shrug.

Sabra wasn't home. That much EV had figured out when the rumbling vehicles failed to bring the Inn owner rushing onto the porch. Lottie Calabrese, who owned the rival establishment across the street, had been peeking out though pristine white curtains ever since they arrived. EV knew phones were buzzing and chirping all over town as Lottie's fingers flew over her messaging app.

"What do you think they'll do if she doesn't come out?"

"She's not in there."

"How could you possibly know that?"

"Trust me, she's on her way. Give it another minute."

"You're a psychic now?" Dalton ran a hand through his hair, fingers snagging in wind-tangled curls.

"Hardly. It doesn't take a psychic to know that we weren't the only ones who saw this caravan of..." words failed her, so she waved a hand to indicate Sabra's visitors, "whatever they are—as it rolled into town. The second that motor home turned down the lane, someone sent out the alert." The words no sooner left her lips than Sabra, carrying a camera and tripod, burst into sight at the far edge of her yard.

"What's going on?" She directed her question toward Dalton; accompanied it with a little swish of the hips. Flirting and breathing were essentially the same thing for Sabra.

"Yeti hunters." EV answered for him. "They're here for you."

"But why?"

"Because you're their queen."

"I'm their what? I don't understand."

Dalton took over. "Apparently your photo has gone viral, and now these people have come to see if they can find Bigfoot. In our town. Or a Yeti. Is there a difference? Either way, they think there's actually a Sasquatch here"

"In our town." EV repeated, emphasized.

"That's so cool." was all Sabra managed before the guy with the camera, having noticed her, rushed over to start asking questions.

"Mrs. Pruitt..."

"Ms." Sabra corrected.

"Ms. Pruitt, please tell us about your experience."

"Well, I was shooting the meteor shower and..."

EV pulled Dalton away. They needed to make some kind of plan for dealing with the situation before it careened any more out of hand. If Sabra's obvious delight at being the center of attention was anything to go by, it might already be too late. EV watched the woman preening in front of the camera; Sabra arched her back enough to make sure her cleavage was shown to perfection before launching into her story with great enthusiasm. She ended with an invitation for those members of the crew who might need lodging to stay at the Inn—at a reduced rate, of course.

"Can't you do something to get them out of here? Maybe tell them they can't interfere with an ongoing investigation."

"They haven't done anything other than talk to Sabra. There's nothing I can do; they're not breaking any laws just by being here."

"So you're not going to do anything?"

"When did I say that? I'm going to have a word with that guy over there," Dalton pointed to an older fellow he'd been watching. While everyone else in the group gathered around the man with the camera, this guy had been checking equipment against a list he carried on a clipboard. Whenever he spoke to one of the crew, that person paid sharp attention; quickly moved to do his bidding.

The guy behind the camera might be the mouth, but this other one was the brains of the operation. Dalton could tell just by looking at him.

Leaving EV to stay or follow, Dalton approached the man with his hand extended.

"Pleased to meet you, Deputy Burnsoll." He gave a firm handshake.

"Jim Dubicki."

Stepping up beside Dalton, EV also shot out a hand, "EV Torrence, what's the plan here, Jim? What exactly is it that you expect to find?" Blunt as ever, she wasn't prepared for his reaction.

Jim's eyes twinkled, his face cracked into a wide grin. "I like a woman who gets right to the point." His up-and-down look made Dalton bristle, and netted him a raised eyebrow from EV, who didn't appreciate the hubris.

"Truth is—I don't expect to find anything here. I think your friend caught a photo of a man creeping through her back yard. There's no Sasquatch in Ponderosa Pines."

"But you believe in Bigfoot?" EV scoffed. Jim shrugged. "No? So why are here?" She questioned.

"We'll be here a few days. You come knock on my door, and I'll show you some pictures that will have you wondering what else is out there." He pointed to the second motor home. "Anytime."

Dalton was ready to reverse his earlier assertion and look for any excuse to run the hunters out of town.

"I'll need to see you gun permits."

"I'd be happy to oblige but we don't have any,"

Dubicki hooked a thumb in his belt loop, "Only thing we're shooting with is cameras."

Swing and a miss. Dalton reconsidered and said, "I can't stop you looking around, but mind the posted land signs. Wear hunter orange when you go into the woods. Wouldn't do to end up the victim of an accidental shooting because you weren't properly outfitted. I'll be keeping a close eye on you..." he gave his fiercest cop face, the one he was learning from Nate, "...and your crew."

Dubicki let the implied threat roll past with only the barest hint of smirk.

EV pulled Dalton toward the car. "Come on, let's leave them to it."

He was quiet all the way back to town.

EV jabbed the #2 key on her cell phone, speed-dialing Chloe as she gunned Christine's engine and headed for home. "What's the haps?" Chloe answered.

EV snorted at Chloe's greeting, a small grin threatening to emerge, even through the fog of irritation in which she was currently mired. "We are being invaded. I repeat—we are being invaded."

"What on earth are you talking about? Sabra's aliens finally touch down? Or... oh, this has to do with our friendly neighborhood Sasquatch, doesn't it?" When it came to putting two and two together, Chloe's mind worked about as fast as EV's, which was one of the things EV loved so much about her.

"Ding. Ding. Ding. You are correct. They're over at the Come On Inn right now—a great big Winnebago full of them—with cameras and microphones, the whole nine. We need to figure out a way to get rid of them; this is not the kind of tourism I'd like to see encouraged around here. We'll have every nutjob in a hundred miles poking their noses into our woods. Damn it, I told Nate this was going to happen."

Silence stretched across the line for a few moments while Chloe pondered the situation. It was a free country; anyone was welcome to come to town, and perhaps they would look around and leave quietly. But she doubted it. The only way to get them to move along was to prove that their 'Bigfoot' was just a mortal man.

"Why don't we just go take a peek in the woods; see for ourselves." Chloe suggested, knowing EV wouldn't turn down a chance to snoop in any form.

"It's a start. And I think we should also do some Internet research; this guy had to come from somewhere. He must have a reason for hiding out in the woods. Someone might be looking for him."

"Yeah, probably wielding a huge butterfly net and a tranquilizer gun."

"So, you'll get started on the research, and tomorrow morning we'll go take a look for ourselves."

"Sounds like a plan. See you tomorrow." Chloe signed off.

Chapter 15

Chloe poked her head through the open top portion of EV's Dutch-style back door, and called out to her friend. "I'm here; let's get this show on the road."

"I'm coming, I'm coming. This whole thing is ludicrous, by the way. They're calling themselves *professional* Yeti hunters. You know every able-bodied male in town has taken a swing through the surrounding woods, and no one has found anything yet." Only EV's voice came to the door; the rest of her was somewhere in the pantry area. Chloe could hear her rummaging around.

EV emerged, sporting a bright orange hat. She handed Chloe an orange vest, holding back a tiny smile at the thought of her friend in hunter's orange. Chloe made a face, but donned the garment. They both knew it was bird hunting season, and weren't taking any chances. EV pulled out Bertha, her trusty

12-gauge shotgun, and strapped it to her back. "Just in case this Sasquatch gets mouthy."

"What crawled up your butt? We know these woods better than most. Those Yeti hunters have no clue. If we can find him first, and prove he's not really Bigfoot, maybe they'll go away and leave us alone." She held up the camera hanging from a strap around her neck for emphasis.

"I like Bertha's odds better, but all right. Let's head to the other side of the pond where the woods are a bit thicker. I'm betting the Sasq-Watchers will poke around Sabras for a while before they take to the more obvious trails. Did you get anywhere on the Inter-webs?"

"Certainly not as far as I'm sure Nate progressed with his official search, but I did read enough about wanted criminals to keep me awake at night. I'll keep digging, but until we have a better description of this whackadoo, it's a crapshoot." EV hadn't really expected a firm lead, but had hoped for a stroke of luck. Maybe their invader didn't hail from nearby. That would make things a lot more difficult.

The two loaded into EV's pickup truck and headed for the canoe launch, opting to take the more scenic—and less frequently traveled—route down a dirt road that wasn't quite wide enough for boat trailers. Sunbeams shone through open spaces in the trees where leaves had recently given up their fight and submitted to unrelenting autumn. Many still clung to life, and some varieties had yet to turn color at all. Fall would continue, with its bursts of yellow, red, and orange for a couple more weeks. Chloe enjoyed the way the plethora of pine trees contributed lush green to the mix of rich colors. It was her favorite time of year, but given everything she'd had on her mind lately, she hadn't much time to enjoy it.

"Your mom and I used to walk this road nearly every day during the summer. We found a *secret garden* back here and claimed it for our own. It was really just a patch of wildflowers in a clearing, but we thought it was beautiful. Later, we brought dates out here before heading out to the pond for some skinny dipping." EV wiggled her eyebrows at Chloe's eye roll and continued. "That's where she and your father kissed for the first time."

Chloe's face softened at the thought of her parents, young and in love, driving out to this spot. She knew Lila had been happy in the Pines once, and she knew that Alexander's death had been the spark that ignited a fire under her mother's butt—sent her careening away from her childhood home. Too young to remember her father, or living at the Pines as a child, his ghost didn't haunt her the way it would have haunted Lila.

Sure, Chloe had spent all her wishes—every shooting star; every birthday candle; every 11:11 on the clock—pleading to have her father back; to know what having a cookie-cutter family would feel like. Just as all children who lost a parent tended to do. But, over time—and as with all things to be endured—the pain diminished to a dull ache, filed away for quiet contemplation. Now, she could observe it without being pulled under by it; whereas Lila couldn't bring herself to speak of Alexander with any semblance of frequency, Chloe enjoyed any tidbit of information she could find.

"Can we look at your photo albums again soon?" Chloe asked EV as they approached their destination.

"Any time you want, Sweets."

EV parked the truck at the end of the road and headed into the woods, following a trail Chloe barely recognized, but that seemed familiar to the older, more seasoned hiker. They trailed around the far side of the pond, covering several miles of ground, and gleaning nothing more than some shots of the brilliant foliage.

"Someone has definitely been through here recently, but with all these fallen leaves I can't track a clear path. It could have been days ago, or even a couple of weeks ago. This is a bust; I say we head back." EV led Chloe back to the truck and hopped in.

"Where else could someone be hiding? Especially someone who's been stockpiling random items pilfered from all around town?"

"I'm not sure, but I think it might be worth a trip to look at the records in the town office. I don't have an updated land survey or topographical map of the Pines, but we can take a look and figure out where the best place to squat might be. What am I missing? I know this area better than most, but I'm coming up blank."

"Drop me here and I'll run over there and meet you back at your place. Got anything good to eat?" Chloe's stomach rumbled.

"It's covered; see you in a bit."

Chloe left the unsightly orange vest in EV's truck, along with her camera bag, and wove through the trail toward the town hall that also held Nate and Dalton's small office. As she approached the edge of the tree line, she noticed a red sports car parked in front of the building. Stopping short, she watched as Nate deposited the same woman from the diner into the driver's seat and waved as she drove away.

Fire burned through Chloe's veins, and steam wanted to pour out of her ears. She felt faint, and angry. Before she even realized what she was doing, Chloe stomped across the street and straight into Nate's office without knocking.

"Who was that? I've seen you with that woman twice now, and I want to know who she is!"

Nate surveyed Chloe for a moment until his own emotions surged up inside him. Part of him was elated; Chloe was jealous, so that must mean she wanted him as more than a friend—while another part of him was angry. Where did she get off acting like he was doing something wrong, when she had been the one gallivanting all over town with the biggest losers EV could find?

Everyone had noticed. Even the gossip-mongering columnist who'd had the audacity to call him *Inspector Hottie*. He was a detective, not an inspector. What an idiot.

"What business is it of yours, anyway? Men have been coming and going from your house so frequently, I was beginning to wonder if you'd taken out a personal ad." He shot back.

"I told you, EV set me up on those dates. I didn't even want to go." Skepticism wrote itself across his face. "What, you don't believe me?"

"I believe you could have said no. I believe you could have told me about it before it happened. You have to know how I feel about you, and it didn't occur to you that maybe that would hurt my feelings?"

Both elation and shame leapt to life within her. Chloe turned her face away, but kept her mouth firmly shut. As much as she wanted to tell him how she felt, she just couldn't find the words. And so far, he hadn't denied that he had been seeing someone else.

The silence stretched out until into its echoing abyss she said, "How? How is it that I *have to know how you feel about me* when you've never told me?"

Looking at him at that particular moment was more than she could do. Whatever emotion might be plastered across his face, she wasn't sure she wanted to know.

In any case, he let the silence lay between them.

"Whatever, *Nathaniel*, you've clearly gotten over

it, so have a nice life!" She spun on her heel and bolted out the door before he could see the tears in her eyes.

The door slammed, and Dalton, who had been standing in the supply closet when Chloe burst in, walked into the room tentatively. "Why didn't you say anything?"

"She's made up her mind, and I'm not going to reward her for coming in here and yelling at me when she's never even let on that she wants more than friendship." Rather than risk making himself vulnerable, Nate had kept his mouth firmly shut, refusing to reveal his true feelings. Maybe he did share some of the blame for all those years of silence, but since his return, he thought he had made his intentions perfectly clear.

He'd battled a bat for her—surely, that was a sign of love. He *had* made his intentions known. Hadn't he? Self-doubt threatened to pull him under, but he ignored its clawing insistence and instead chose to remain indignant.

"You're being stubborn, and short-sighted. I know you love her, and you could be throwing away the best thing that ever happened to you." Dalton hoped his friend would see reason, but knew enough not to push too hard.

"My personal business is none of your concern. Get back to work." Nate said sullenly. Dalton nodded, beat back the temptation to smack the young idiot in the back of the head, and decided to put a pin in the conversation, at least for the time being.

Outside, Chloe took a deep breath before trudging back through the woods toward EV's, her mission at the town office unfulfilled and forgotten.

Chapter 16

Wind whistled and shrieked through Ponderosa Pines, stripping early-turned trees of their fall glory, and sending them skittering into every corner. EV fought to keep the lumbering pickup from being blown off track on her way into town. By the time she muscled her way to the curb, she was wishing she'd stayed home.

The promise of gossip had dragged her from the warmth of her cozy fortress, and the stress of the drive turned her feet toward where dark-brewed, caffeine-laced nectar waited.

There was time for a cup before knitting group. EV pushed the coffee shop door open. Struggling, she managed to get halfway in before the wind sucked it closed again. So she shoved harder. The wind died down long enough to let the door slam open hard. EV stumbled through, and grasped the edge of the closest table to catch herself from falling.

Unfortunately, her knitting bag suffered no such reprieve, and flew out of her hand to dump its contents all over the floor. Muttering imprecations under her breath, EV gathered the mess together without bothering with neatness, and shoved it back into her bag.

Combing her fingers through her hair, EV tried to restore some semblance of order to the tumbled mass. Failing miserably, she fell into her customary chair with a whooshing breath.

"Blustery out, hmm?" She said to Rhonda, who approached with a coffee pot and mug.

"You should hear the wind whistling out the back door. It's crazy." Rhonda agreed. Glancing around to make sure no one was close enough to hear, she lowered her voice to a whisper. "And speaking of crazy, listen to what happened this morning."

EV gestured for Rhonda to sit.

"You remember that table and chair that was taken from here? Well, they're back."

"The thief returned them?" Unexpected news.

"Yeah, but he didn't simply return them, he

repaired them and then, well, you have to see for yourself. Come on."

Rhonda led EV behind the counter and through a door leading out the back of the shop.

"Look."

The only reason EV knew they were the same pieces of furniture that had gone missing was that they matched the rest of the tables in the shop in both size and shape. But that was where the resemblance ended.

If their invader was a Sasquatch, he sure knew how to work a penknife. How long it had taken to carve the name of the shop, along with a finely nuanced, steaming mug surrounded by coffee beans, EV couldn't speculate. Horizontal stripes of black and white decorated the rim of the table—courtesy of the school's missing art supplies, EV supposed. Matching stripes decorated the seat rim, and back of the chair.

"We found them outside the back door this morning when we opened up the shop. David said not to touch them because they'd probably be considered evidence."

"And nobody saw anything?" EV appraised the pieces as best she could—from a distance, and with the wind still whipping her hair into her eyes.

The round cafe table, meant for a single diner, or maybe a couple if they wanted to get cozy, would easily fit in the wheelbarrow that had been stolen from Horis. And with a little rope to secure it, the chair, too.

Pulling out her phone, EV snapped a few photos, and though she suspected David had already done so, advised Rhonda to alert Nate or Dalton to this new development. No sense in keeping them in the dark, but if Rhonda did the calling, EV wouldn't be asked to share her thoughts on who might be behind the thefts—and now the non-thefts.

She had plenty of thoughts. Nebulous ones that she couldn't seem to marshal into any type of pattern. And right now, it was time for knitting group —providing anyone else had braved the wild weather.

When EV blew—literally—into Thread, the shop next door that hosted knitting group, she grinned to see that it was as full, as always. Ponderosa Pines bred hardiness into its citizens—to them, a little wind was an inconvenience, not an excuse for hibernating.

That the ongoing discussion had not become hushed at her appearance, coupled with the enthusiastic greeting she received, convinced EV she had been worried over nothing when she speculated about being cut out of the gossip loop. She laid it down to the craziness present around harvest time, and the inevitable rush of getting ready for winter.

Choosing a seat on the sofa, EV reached into her bag to pull out the mangled mass of yarn and needles she had shoved in there scant minutes before. Priscilla Lewellyn, owner of Thread, and leader of the group—a woman whose features and movements always reminded EV of a chicken—actually enhanced that mental image by clucking when she saw the mess.

Oh, well. EV was never going to make a star knitter, as anyone who had ever received one of her scarves for Christmas could attest. She had absolutely no patience for it. But, coming here kept her in touch with her neighbors. So she would continue to knit parallelogram-shaped afghans and scarves with wobbly, uneven edges, and maybe this year she would even attempt a hat.

An ugly one, no doubt. Mainly because Priscilla flatly refused to sell EV any of the prettier, more expensive yarns until she at least learned the purl stitch. If the refusal had been meant to spark EV on to greater heights of learning, it had failed, utterly.

After watching EV fumble helplessly while trying to untangle the wind-tossed mess of yarn, Priscilla, with an uncharacteristically sharp gesture, snatched the bundle from EV's hands and began to sort it out herself. Apparently, her unlimited patience did have a breaking point. Under Priscilla's deft hands, the yarn was quickly untangled. Noting a dropped stitch or two, she took the time to weave them back in before returning the work to its owner. Priscilla's stern look made EV long to stick out her tongue.

Allegra Worth, the woman whose husband—soon-to-be ex—had killed Evan Plunkett, sat apart from the rest and knitted quietly. In the weeks since Ashton had gone to prison, she'd begun to take on a softer—less Cruella DeVille—look.

Town consensus, among those who hypothesized about such things—which was nearly everyone—had pegged her as likely to slink out of town in the middle of the night. Yet, here she was. Calmly knitting. EV had to give the woman credit for having guts enough to stay. More, for showing up here, knowing Talia Plunkett rarely missed a session.

Talia, sister-in-law to the philandering Evan, and

wife of Luther, put on a cheerful front, but EV noted the occasional flick of her eyes toward Allegra. Nothing the shift of her shoulders away from Allegra's side of the room, and the tinge of color in her cheeks, EV concluded that Talia wasn't completely comfortable being in the same room with the woman whose affair had been at the heart of her own husband's murder. Who could blame Talia for that? EV, for one, admired her restraint, and her hardy constitution; a lesser woman would have torn Allegra's hair out by the roots.

Talk turned to the recent rash of thefts.

"I haven't been able to find my Uno cards for a month." Talia pitched her voice low and ominous.

"Crying out loud, Talia," Lottie chided, her voice shrill with derision. "Unless you left them outside, they're probably safe." The look she gave her sister included plenty of scorn, along with a set of rolling eyes, and garnered her a scorching glance from Talia.

"You don't know. Those pictures Sabra took face right at my bedroom window. We, the whole town, rarely ever lock our doors, so he could have been creeping around in my house."

"Yes, I'm sure there's a big black market for stolen Uno cards."

Before the sisters came to blows, EV figured she'd better do something to distract them.

"Last night he brought back the table he took from out behind The Mudbucket." EV tossed the comment into the mix.

"Really?" Wide eyes and perked ears turned toward EV.

"And you should see what he did to it. He fixed it, and carved a design into the top. It's beautiful work."

"So our thief is also an artist?"

"Looks that way. It's an art attack."

"Say what you want about him, but I know he took my Englebert, and Drambuie is missing besides."

"Cats?" Priscilla questioned.

"Englebert is my ceramic gargoyle and Drambuie is that white cat I found the night Luther died. He's such a darling. I hope that nasty thief hasn't eaten him."

"Oh, Lottie, that's disgusting," Talia shivered at the thought, "Don't even say such a thing."

Chapter 17

He should have taken the truck. That was the uppermost thought in Dalton's mind after two minutes spent battling the wind that whipped hair into his eyes with great ferocity. Already halfway to The Mudbucket, it was nearly as much trouble to go back as it was to go forward. He dodged left to take shelter in the recessed doorway of the co-op.

Throughout the summer months, the co-op ran three days a week. Everyone who wished to participate, from full-time farmers to hobby growers used the facility as a place to buy, sell, and trade their crops with other co-op members. Part of the payment came through sweat equity. In order to become a co-op member, one must commit to a certain amount of time spent harvesting or packing crops. Anything extra was sold at the weekly farmer's market, which drew buyers from both inside and outside Ponderosa Pines.

Sheltered, somewhat from the wind, Dalton reached for his phone; opened the latest email forwarded from Nate's private investigator friend. His thumbs flew over the phone's touchscreen. Remy Vincent. Acid swirled through Dalton's stomach in the seconds before it dropped like a broken elevator into his shoes. He'd hoped the tip would lead to a dead end, but according to Nate, it was nearly a lock for Vincent having some part in the blackmail attempt on Evan Plunkett.

The passage of time had done nothing to dull Dalton's dislike of the strutting little peacock he remembered. Brutally self-aware, Dalton knew that jealousy played more than a small part in his utter contempt for the other man. Unlike Remy, Dalton had never felt that the measure of a man rested in the number of greenbacks he carried in his wallet. Or for that matter, anything he carried in his pants—and Dalton knew his pants were more loaded in every way.

And still, Vincent had gotten the girl. What had EV seen in that jerk?

It occurred to him that part of his anger at Remy

had to do with thinking less of EV for being fooled. Admitting that to himself wasn't his finest moment. Admitting it to her was not in the cards. Ever.

Dalton felt the slow burn that always accompanied thoughts of how the shallow teen had pulled the wool over EV's eyes. Even under the facade of distance she maintained at times, EV, at heart, was a rampant idealist—and Ponderosa Pines was her vision of utopia. One that Dalton saw as clearly as she did. One that Remy decried at every turn.

Friends, families, and townspeople all working together toward the common goal of treading lightly on the earth made for an intimate community. One where help, a drink of water, or a sympathetic ear waited behind every door in town—sometimes whether you wanted them or not.

In his new capacity as Deputy, Dalton saw the reports—the BOLOs, the Amber Alerts—and felt sorrow for anyone who would never know the kind of safety and support that had marked his childhood.

Evan Plunkett's murder had taken some of the innocence from this town. Given the chance, Remy Vincent would strip it to the bone. Dalton decided it could not be allowed to happen.

Not on his watch.

If EV's heart sped up a little when she noticed Dalton standing in the shaded alcove, she was more disturbed by the feeling of warmth that stole over her at the mere sight of him—at the way her fingers itched to touch his arm, his hair, his face.

Sentimental slob, she accused herself. *Get a grip.*

Still, she leaned into the wind to cross the narrow street.

Absorbed in rereading Nate's report, and deafened by the shriek of the wind, he hadn't heard her coming, and so jumped when EV burst into the sheltered lee of the doorway.

In a guilty rush, he pocketed his phone before EV could make out anything on the screen.

Ignoring her tilted-head appraisal and narrowed eyes, Dalton said, "Nasty breeze today." He nearly had to shout for her to hear him above the unrelenting drone of air brushing past buildings, through trees.

"Always the king of understatement," she pitched her voice above the din.

White teeth flashed at her before he laid an arm around her shoulders, pulled her in next to him to watch Allegra Worth fight her way toward the Jeep she had recently traded for Ashton's car. A short struggle with the door had Dalton tense in preparation to go help, but with a mighty wrench, Allegra managed to cram herself and her knitting bag safely inside with the door firmly closed. But not before a loud burst of unsavory language wafted above the sound of the wind to where EV and Dalton stood.

"Inventive." EV approved. Sometimes there was no substitute for a good bout of cussing. The Jeep made a tight U-turn, before speeding past as a particularly violent gust of wind sent a spate of wet leaves flying toward where the pair sheltered. Another gust stole the laughter, and then the breath from Dalton while he picked leaves from EV's hair; let the silky strands slide through his fingers.

"Come on," EV strode toward her truck. "Get in," she gestured toward the passenger's door.

Inside, the noise level dropped by enough that the sudden lack of intermittent screaming felt like cotton in EV's ears. "Gonna be trees down all over town if this keeps up."

When the comment garnered her no more than a mumble, EV turned in the seat to face Dalton; searched his face for some clue to his thoughts.

"What's crawled up your backside?"

"Remy Vincent."

EV paled. "Must be a tight fit." Maybe a joke would lighten the moment.

Or maybe not.

"What was the big attraction? It's been thirty years and you're still pining away for that weasel."

Pining away? Is that what he thought she was doing? EV pressed a finger to the temple that had begun to throb the minute she'd heard him say that name. A hot retort sprang to her lips. She bit it back while contemplating how it must look to him.

"It's not like that." Her feeble attempt at an explanation elicited a snort from him.

"Then how is it?"

How could she explain to the man what it had been like to feel the life she carried slip away in a wash of pain and blood? How she had mourned when the doctor explained that the fetus was no longer viable? No longer viable. The clinical way of saying *your baby is dead*. And it was a baby; no technical terminology changed that bare fact. Her son was much more than simply a mass of tissue, viable or not—and he was dead. Gone forever.

Fast as a joyless breath.

Even before that moment, her love for Remy had fled. In the aftermath of the miscarriage, he represented nothing more to her than the source of pain so immense it swallowed her whole. No, it was not Remy that she mourned. Never Remy. But her heart would keen for her son until her last breath let her join him.

Was she ready to lay that pain before Dalton? There had never been another man she trusted enough to share her secret—was he the one?

He felt like the one, and that scared her more than anything.

"Why are you asking about this now?"

See, that little voice inside her shouted, *this is why we don't get into relationships. Too many emotional pitfalls.*

She watched his eyes slide away from hers as though he had something to hide.

"Do you have any idea what the blackmailer had on Evan?" The abrupt change of subject staggered EV.

"I...no. What?" Off balance, she tried to wrap her mind around the question.

"The blackmailer had leverage. Figuring out that leverage might give us a connection to his identity."

Honestly, the man flip-flopped faster than a champion pancake turner. Unless...

Was there some connection between Remy and

the blackmailer? No, there couldn't be. Remy had not been back to Ponderosa Pines since the day he'd left her.

"Is there something you need to tell me, Dalton?"

"No." He was lying. No question about it.

"If I think of anything, I'll let you know." She turned the key, nodding her head toward the door to indicate his dismissal. When he didn't move, she said, "If you don't mind, I'll be on my way."

"EV, I..." He cut off the words, exited the truck without slamming the door—though he was mightily tempted—and, leaning into the wind, walked in the opposite direction while she drove away.

All he wanted to do was get back to his office; slam some file drawers until he felt better. Fate was not so kind. He made it as far as the coffee shop, where Rhonda wrenched open the door.

"Dalton, I've been trying to call you." He pulled out his phone to see he'd missed two of her calls.

"What can I do for you?"

"I need to show you something." She led him out the back to see the returned table.

Chapter 18

Rock music with a heavy beat poured out of the speakers while EV kicked and pummeled the punching bag hanging from her bedroom rafters. Jab—jab—kick. Kick—jab—kick. She fell into the rhythm of the music and the motion.

She needed the physical outlet to help clear her head.

All this Dalton business had pulled her into the mire that she had managed to avoid for most of her adult life. Love was fine for teenagers, but it didn't last. People let you down in the worst ways, and at the worst times.

If things had gone differently, today she might be celebrating something wonderful rather than trying to distract herself with exercise.

She punched the bag again, harder and harder, but the memories still came. Maybe it was time to tell

Chloe her secret. Tears spilled to mingle with the rivulets of sweat running down her face as she battered the bag; battered her past.

An hour passed before she found any peace; before she was too tired to rage.

EV slipped into the shower, cranked the water on hot, and let it pound on her.

She'd just stepped out of the steamy bathroom when the phone rang.

Ignore it.

It kept ringing. The machine must be off.

Whoever it was, they were persistent.

For no other reason than to stop the annoying sound, EV picked up the receiver.

"Hello."

"Hey Sweetpea." One person in the world called her that and lived to tell the tale. Lila.

"How's life in the jet-set lane?"

"It's fine. I'm fine." Lila was quiet for so long EV wondered why she'd bothered to call if she didn't want to talk.

"Chloe's doing fine. We had a little excitement around...."

Lila cut her off. "EV, I...I need to tell you something. I ran into Remy the other day. He asked about you."

What was it with his name popping up time after time lately?

"He's...he...what?"

"He asked a bunch of questions—is she married? Did she have kids? Is she happy? Things like that."

"What did you tell him?"

"I told him the truth. And I told him I thought you were seeing someone. What was I supposed to do?"

"Nothing." EV felt a sinking sensation in her gut. His being back in her life in any capacity right now was the last thing she needed. "You don't think he'll come here, do you?"

"Wouldn't that be a good thing? Give you some closure. You're not still in love with him so... Wait. You're not still in love with him, right?"

"No, of course not." Not even a little bit. What's more, comparing the way she felt about Remy to what she had begun to feel for Dalton, she was starting to see that her feelings for Remy had been little more than the shallow ghost of love.

"Good. Because for all his concern, he gave me the vibe."

"Vibe?"

"That niggling feeling he's up to something slimy. He made a snide remark about you living in the boonies."

"Well, you'd be the authority on hating the Pines." It was a bitterly passive-aggressive accusation, and EV wasn't proud of having made it.

Still the barb struck home.

"I don't hate the town." Lila said with a catch in her voice.

"We're a pair, aren't we? Both running from bad memories. Chloe is blossoming here. You should be proud of her. I am."

"She's happy, then? What about the Harper boy? She talks about him, and I can tell there's something there."

"Stubborn fools—the pair of them. He's head over heels for her, and she lights up like Christmas around him, but they're having trouble getting out of the friend-zone. It'll come right in the end. What about you? Anyone special?"

"Yes. A lovely man who has swept me off my feet." Lila had always attracted the type of man prone to dramatic romantic gestures. "I think he might be the one."

That's new.

"Do tell. I didn't think you were shopping in the *forever* store these days."

"I'm not. I wasn't." Lila continued telling EV all about the man in her life who sounded too good to be true. "...I think he might propose."

"And if he does?"

"I'm going to accept. I feel giddy as a schoolgirl."

"Have you talked to Chloe?" Probably not, since Chloe would have told EV if she thought Lila was in a serious relationship.

"She knows I'm seeing someone." Lila hedged.

"But not that it's serious. You need to tell her."

"I did. I think she figured it was just another one of my flings. She gave me one of her patented indulge-the-crazy lady responses, so I dropped the subject. Maybe you could talk to her...soften her up to the idea."

"No. You know I love you both as if you were my own blood, but this is between you and her. Deal with it Lila, and soon."

"I will. What do you want me to do if Remy comes around again?"

"Tell him I moved on."

"Have you?"

"From him? A long time ago. He's not the reason I've stayed single. Now I'm in something...I guess you could call a relationship."

"With Dalton Burnsoll? Chloe filled me in."

"He's...it's complicated."

"See, that's where you get into trouble, EV. You over-think things. Love shouldn't be so complicated and angst-y. You need to get out of your own way. Dalton's a good man—he's not Remy."

"No. He's not."

"Does he give you the fluttery feeling?"

"Yeah." EV made it sound like a bad thing.

"Have you slept with him?"

"No."

"That tells me you do have feelings for him."

"I already told you, it's complicated. He's hiding something from me."

"That wasn't a no, which means you do care for him, and now you're looking for an excuse to push him away. Don't you think what he's hiding might be related his job? Maybe it's not that he *won't* tell you but that he *can't*. Either way, if you love the man, why don't you just tell him? What's holding you back?"

"I don't know. Nothing. Everything."

"It's okay to fall, as long as there's someone there to catch you."

"Don't wait so long to call again." EV was finished with the subject of her love life. "Maybe come for a visit sometime."

Lila wasn't quite ready to let it go. "The day you marry Dalton Burnsoll—that's the day I'll come back."

Chapter 19

This time, when Nate stepped in front of the elders' chamber, he wasn't nervous. In fact, he was incensed. When Elise's ill-timed visit netted him the name of one of Ponderosa Pines' esteemed elders in connection with Remy Vincent, he couldn't believe it. The doors opened; he strode inside with purpose, and stood at the head of the table to address the six individuals sitting before him. Dalton, who had chosen to accompany Nate, stayed quiet, but remained at his side in a show of support.

"Hello, all of you." He looked at each in turn before settling his gaze on Marjorie Hillard. "I know the last time we spoke, you asked us to stop investigating the origin of the blackmail notes sent to Evan Plunkett. I'm not sorry to say that we didn't listen. A contact of mine has come back with a name: Remy

Vincent. And it's come to my attention that he is your nephew, Marjorie."

The blank look on Marjorie's face threw Nate off; he was a good cop, and was surprised at her composure. Typically, when someone was about to get busted for passing information to a criminal, their expression showed some level of panic or nervousness. Marjorie appeared perfectly at ease.

"Remy's behind the threats against Evan—that much we know. But what we couldn't figure out was how he obtained inside information; the blackmailer knew too much, too soon, to not have had an accomplice in town. Marjorie, we know you have been in contact with your nephew. Have you been reporting to him in order to sabotage the town?"

Emotion definitely showed in her face now; it had gone from surprise, to pain, to indignation during Nate's speech.

"Of course, I'm not trying to sabotage the town! I helped build this town; helped turn it into what it is today. I would never do anything to bring harm upon us. I can't believe this. Remy is a good man."

"Marjorie, he's not. We have several witnesses who have identified him as the man who attended the Gilmore town meeting, and pitched the idea of a merger. Did you know about that?"

"I had no idea Remy was in the area. Or that he made the proposal. He never let on that he had any ill intentions toward the Pines. Yes, when he left, twenty-odd years ago, he made it clear he didn't enjoy living here, and would be moving on. Lately, though, he seemed to soften." Marjorie's eyes flicked back and forth while she searched her memory for an indication that Remy was up to no good. When she rested her elbows on the table and placed her finger-tips to her temples, Nate knew she had come to a difficult conclusion.

"We speak on the phone regularly, and now I realize he was pumping me for information. I never thought much of it. After all, he used to live here; he had friends and family here. What will happen to him? What kind of charges is he facing?"

"Marjorie, we're going to have to pursue this to the fullest extent of the law. After all, if Ashton hadn't known Evan was being blackmailed, Evan might still be alive."

Nate studied Marjorie's face, and though she could be lying about the nature of her involvement with Remy, he didn't think it was likely. Besides, continuing a witch hunt would certainly tick off the rest of the elders. He softened slightly at the elderly woman's obvious angst.

"This all makes more sense, and is actually quite a relief. I'm sorry I came on so strong—bad cop, you know."

Edward Burnsoll spoke up. "I always thought he had a few issues, Margie. It's not so surprising. We all know you would never intentionally give out information you thought was sensitive. Why do you suppose he's so filled with hate?"

"Yes, he's always been an odd duck, a little big for his britches. He had me thinking he missed living in the Pines." A spark of annoyance lit inside her. "He said he couldn't face coming back to the place where his parents lived, not even to come clean out their house; I had to go through all my sister's personal belongings. I had some help, but it was painful, and he should have taken on some of the responsibility. Remy didn't stand to gain anything by making us merge with Gilmore, as far as I can see. I'd very much like to know what his motive is. It can't be money; he doesn't need it."

"You understand what this investigation will entail, don't you?" Dalton finally spoke. Everyone looked around the table at each of their comrades, all eyes finally settled on Marjorie.

"Yes, I understand. I want you to do your job; no matter what. I'll cooperate in any way I can. Make sure he doesn't have another opportunity to wreak havoc. I'll continue to talk to him like nothing is amiss, but I'm not going to give him any real information. If there's anything I can do, maybe pass along a bit of falsehood to help you out, let me know."

Nate felt the weight of what was to come, for him and for Dalton, and most of all for Marjorie, who had just lost faith in a family member. "Do you know where he is?" Nate asked gently.

"I'm guessing you already have the phone number he calls me from. He doesn't ever send me anything through the mail. He did mention he'd be taking a trip soon; warned me I might not hear from him for a couple of weeks. But I doubt it will be long, if he's still trying to keep tabs on the goings-on around here. He mentioned France, but who knows if he was telling me the truth."

Johnathan Lewellyn stood, signaling the end of the conversation. "You have our full support, Nathaniel. Do what you need to do, and keep us informed. I can't say how sorry I am that we didn't listen to you the first time. The fact that we're being targeted by a relative insider—a former resident—changes things significantly. If he's still stewing after all these years, he won't stop now."

"Thank you, we'll make sure you're updated on our progress."

"Now, about those Sasq-Watchers...."

Chapter 20

Feet propped on an upturned log, in front of the roaring campfire, EV wondered how her backside could still be cold, while the bits of her that faced the blazing flames were far enough past toasty and heading into scorched territory. She dumped the last splash of hot chocolate mixed with cinnamon Schnapps from the thermos into her cup, slugged half the contents, and felt the heat hit her belly.

So rarely did EV drink more than a single glass of wine with a meal, that this second thermos of laced chocolate loosened her tongue and made her tipsy.

"Tell me how it's going with you and Dalton. There's more of a vibe there for you than I've ever seen you have with anyone else." Chloe probed gently. They made a good couple, whether EV wanted to admit it or not.

"I don't know. We've been friends forever, so it

feels funny thinking about him that way." EV tossed a twig toward the flames, while Chloe twirled a marshmallow on a stick to get that perfectly browned coating. "He wants more than I can give."

"Why? You're not exactly an old woman. And I know firsthand how compassionate and caring you are. Why do you hold yourself back from caring for him? I think you'd be so good together. He makes you laugh."

"I was engaged once."

"To Remy? My mom mentioned him."

"She didn't tell you the whole story, because she doesn't know it. No one does."

Chloe waited quietly, in case asking questions spooked EV into clamming up again.

"Remy and your mom were my best friends. We were like a team, inseparable." She paused long enough that Chloe began to think EV might not finish her story.

"Mom said the same thing."

"I never noticed... I was young and naive, totally inexperienced with dating or romance. Backwards, really. So, when he started falling for me, I was completely oblivious. Then, when he finally kissed me, I was scared to death. I think my hormones took a lot longer to kick in than most people's do. But when they did, I was sunk. I fell headlong. So hard that it felt I'd died and come back to life in a new world. His world. I lost myself in it, and it was everything. He felt the same, or I thought he did."

Chloe had an inkling of how that felt, but she could tell it had been stronger with EV.

"We made plans for a life together, picked out a plot of land where we would build our house, even chose names for the babies we would have." She sipped at the sweet, spicy drink. "It was all a mask that started slipping after he visited his grandparents that first time. When he came back, he picked at me; at your mother; at life in Ponderosa Pines."

"His grandparents' influence?"

"Seemed like. We fought, and I broke it off with him. This town—what it is now; what we've built here—this was my parent's dream to begin with. I think it passed to me through their blood, because it also became mine. As much as I loved him, I couldn't let him take that away from me."

This was not news to Chloe; she'd seen firsthand the passion EV had for her home.

After a moment, EV continued, "After a few weeks, he came to his senses. We reconciled. I thought we were stronger than ever; happier than ever. The next summer, he kept a lid on his attitude, so we stayed strong. We were accepted to the same school, as planned. We moved into off-campus housing. It was like a dream." There was another pause, and when her voice floated toward Chloe again, it was pensive.

"A month before graduation, I found out I was pregnant—six weeks along." EV ignored Chloe's sharp intake of breath. Or maybe she didn't even hear it. What she did hear, though, were the angry voices from her past. The recriminations from Remy that she had jumped ahead of their carefully laid out plans; the distance that he put between them with his anger; the names he called her, and finally, several weeks later, the gentle voice of the ER doctor who told her she'd lost the baby.

The way Remy flipped after that—acted as though he had wanted nothing more than to father a child; as though she had done something purposefully to lose the baby. After that, another about face. With bewildering harshness, Remy's parting shot was that at least, now, he was free to go make something out of himself.

He'd had the decency to help her move back

home; to bring her baby there to rest before he left; to see that she was comfortable and to never—her parting request to him—tell anyone about the baby, or what had happened between them.

Those were the ghosts that haunted EV's past, and she laid them before Chloe with carefully chosen words while Chloe's tears fell like rain.

"It was the baby—my son—who took my heart when he left, because—by then—Remy had already lost it, along with my respect."

Chloe could find no soothing words to spread over the wound. All she could do was pull EV into a fierce hug that lasted long minutes, while EV finally shed the hardest tears Chloe had ever seen from her.

When EV stopped trembling, Chloe gave her one last squeeze.

"You have to tell Dalton."

EV's eyebrows launched into her hairline. "I have to what? Why?"

"Tell Dalton." Chloe tossed a couple more small logs onto the fire; poked it back to life. She turned her chair sideways toward it, so she could watch EV's face in the glow of the flames. What she needed to say would require tact and diplomacy. "He deserves to know what it is that's coming between you."

As expected, EV's brow furrowed into mutinous lines. "What business is it of his?"

"Well, duh. He's in love with you, for one. And for two, he thinks you're still in love with Remy, and that's why you hold him at arm's length. It's not fair. I'm sorry, but it's not." She clarified, when EV threw her a dirty look.

"He's a great guy, and he's worth you getting out of that rut—even if I have to kick you out of there myself." Her tone turned gentle. "You have so much to give, and you deserve someone who understands that. Especially after such a profound loss."

All expression left EV's face like someone dropped a shutter over it, and Chloe realized that half the problem lay in the fact that EV blamed herself for losing the baby. She stood in the way of her own happiness.

"You know that, right? That it wasn't your fault."

"Shut up." EV muttered sullenly.

"I will not." Chloe wasn't sure she had ever felt so indignant for—and at—someone at the same time. "You weren't to blame. These things happen sometimes, and it's nobody's fault. Least of all yours and I bet that's what the doctor told you, too."

"She did."

"Don't you think it's time you let yourself off the hook?"

"Shut up," EV repeated.

"You know I'll take this to my grave. But if you don't tell him, you'll always wonder what might have happened. Don't go there, EV. Let him in."

A few minutes later, when EV seemed likely to never speak again, Chloe dropped a kiss on her head and disappeared inside.

Chapter 21

Still sitting where Chloe had left her, EV skewered one last marshmallow; held it over the coals to roast, until it reached the peak of toasty goodness on the outside and melting creaminess on the inside. A few seconds too long, and she'd lose it to the fire—not long enough, and there would be a big blob of solid matter in the middle.

The simple act helped settle something inside her, and in the calmness, she realized that the voice in her head—the one full of recrimination for the lost life she'd held inside—had gone silent for the first time she could remember. Sharing her secret had lightened its burden on her soul.

The second she popped the morsel of perfection into her mouth, she heard Dalton's truck turn down her road. Anticipation sent a flutter through her belly as she recognized the throaty purr of his engine.

Stop acting like a teenager, she chided herself. *You keep this up, you'll get pimples.*

She listened for the slamming of his door; his steps down the stone walkway. Before he could knock, she called to him. "Come around back."

"Coming."

He settled into Chloe's hot pink camp chair; the dancing light coming off the glowing embers cast his face into partial shadow, though EV could still see his wry grin. Pink was so not his color—a nice pastel purple would suit him better.

Since she was within reaching distance, he reached; curled his fingers over hers.

The companionable silence lasted a few minutes before he spoke into the flickering night.

"We need to talk."

His words turned the flutter in her belly from gentle butterfly touches to the wrenching feeling that comes right before a fall. This was about to become too much honesty for one night.

"The four words no one in a relationship ever wants to hear."

"Are we?"

He took her silence for confusion. "In a relationship, I mean."

"Yes...no—it's complicated."

"Not for me. I'm not a complicated guy with some dire secret in my past that keeps me from trusting anyone ever again. Not that there's anything wrong with that," he amended quickly, when he felt tension clench her hand where it lay beneath his.

"How do you do it, Dalton? After Marlene betrayed you like that—how do you have the courage to try again?"

"How do you have the courage to face everything alone?"

"Touché."

"EV, I'm not going to grovel. I won't be another notch on your headboard." Residual anger from having to talk about Remy Vincent all day gave his words more weight than he intended. They slapped and stung. EV's mouth went dry. She slammed her inner walls into place.

"Wow, Dalton. Tell me how you really feel. Why are you so hung up on me if you think I'm a slut?"

He hadn't meant it that way.

"Did I say that? I don't think I said that." Yet, he knew the implications were there. "I meant that I'm not the one night stand kind of guy." As the words left his mouth, he knew he had made it worse.

"Excuse me?"

"I wish I'd worn different boots—be easier to pry my foot out of my mouth if I had on something in a rounder toe."

A snort of laughter escaped before EV could stop it. Self-deprecating wit always scored high with her. His brand of humor fit perfectly into that category.

"Probably go down better with a side of crow."

"Would that be fried crow? Or baked?"

"Well," EV considered, "you could just stuff it."

She gave back as good as she got.

Dalton rose from the pink chair to toss more wood onto the dying fire. He'd dug himself a deep enough hole that they might be there awhile, and the action gave him time to carefully plan his next words.

He sat back down, stretched his feet out toward the flames, listening to the crackle and sizzle of burning pine for several moments before he spoke, "I have feelings for you, Emmalina." Her name sounded like a caress. The simplicity of his confession touched something inside her. "But I'm willing to walk away if you tell me you'll never feel the same—if there's no chance for us."

As he said it, she could picture it; a life without

him in it—it wasn't difficult to do; she'd had plenty of practice. Years and years of it.

EV tipped her head back, let her eyes drop shut. Moving forward meant laying her deepest secret at his feet. Her instincts told her he could handle it; that he would pick up the burden of her past, and carry it with him. Telling him would lighten the weight as much as telling Chloe had. Maybe more.

Telling him would lay open the wound, and let it finally heal.

Mistaking her silence for something other than it was Dalton assumed the worst.

"I see." Bleak, bitter pain rose in him. It was over before it had even begun.

"No, you really don't."

"Really? Tell me you see some kind of future for us, Emmalina. Say the words."

"I want to be with you, Dalton." She would not stoop to the convenient lie; but still, she wasn't sure she was ready to rip off the Band-Aid time had laid over her soul; to expose the throbbing sore.

"But..." He prompted.

"But what?"

"There's a *but.*"

"No, there's not. There's something I need to tell you about."

A soft pop sounded when a log burned apart; sending a shower of sparks skyward.

EV gathered herself to speak. "I know you think Remy broke my heart. It wasn't him. It was losing my —our—son." For the second time that night, she told the whole story.

Whatever he had expected to hear, this bombshell was nowhere on the list. Sympathy moved his hand to reach, again, for hers; to squeeze.

"I'm sorry for your loss." The words were inadequate; sounded trite to his ears. Marlene had given him Carrie. He would never forget the utter joy of watching his only daughter come into the world; of hearing her first cry; feeling her tiny fingers instinctively clutch his own. Trying to imagine having that joy ripped away from him hurt enough that compassion for EV overwhelmed him.

"No one knows. And before you ask, I don't know why I've kept it a secret."

"Don't you?" The flash of anger surprised him. "Saint Emmalina, carries the world on her shoulders and thinks she's doing everyone a favor." His inner response echoed Chloe's earlier.

His heart was breaking for her while at the same time, he wanted to strangle her. The stubborn woman.

His words fell like stones upon her; sent bitter tears to sting and burn.

"Low blow."

Now he'd made her cry. Dalton launched from the chair to stalk the perimeter of the fire like a caged beast.

"Denying the people who love you the chance to support you when you are hurting isn't a sign of strength. You do them a disservice."

"That was never my intention." How could he be slapping at her after she'd bared her soul to him? And worse, what if he was right? She could see it now—how protecting her loved ones from another loss had taken something from them.

"I've been a fool." The quiet sadness broke something in him, let the anger drain away. Dalton pulled EV from the chair and into his arms; ran his hands down her back to soothe away the tension.

"Let me love you, EV. Let me hold you when it hurts. Don't shut me out." Dalton leaned back, lifted a hand to cup her chin, angled her face until their eyes met. Everything he felt for her was there, lit by the flickering flames of the dying fire; he held nothing back.

All her carefully built walls came crashing down. She let them fall to rubble at his feet; let him see her vulnerable and needing. EV whispered his name.

He kissed her. Gently at first. Nothing more than a brush of firm lips against her own.

Everything inside her surged toward him, a tsunami of pent up emotion that hit him, dragged him under as she took the kiss from gentle to urgent.

"Come," EV broke the kiss, and leaving the fire to burn to ash, pulled him toward her house; her bed.

The feeling that someone was watching her woke EV from a sound sleep the next morning. Dalton had been watching her sleep. Normally, that would have creeped her out, but today, it made her feel cherished. She smiled back at him, stretched, and tangled her legs with his.

"Did you know you hum in your sleep?" He found it charming.

"I do not." Did she?

"It's cute."

Brushing sleep-mussed hair away from her face, his breath caught. "Just look at you." He leaned in to kiss her when his phone signaled an incoming call.

He muttered an oath; reached over to retrieve the beeping annoyance from his pants pocket.

"Burnsoll." Whatever he heard on the other end triggered a sidelong glance at EV. Dalton slid from the bed, pulled on a pair of bright purple, jersey boxers that any other time might have made EV grin. Not now, though. Now, she knew he was trying to hide something from her.

Running through the possibilities, she dismissed another woman. Juggling females had never been Dalton's style. Maybe it was something to do with Carrie. Nothing he said gave her any clue. His end of the conversation consisted of a series of *yeps* and *nopes*. EV sat up in the bed, wrapped the sheet tightly around her, and listened shamelessly.

When Dalton keyed off his phone, he carefully blanked his expression before turning back to where EV lay watching him with those whiskey-colored eyes of hers that always saw too much.

"Work stuff," was his brief comment. His glance moved from his pants back to the bed as though unsure whether to get dressed or climb back in with her. EV shuttered her emotions; gave him a smile that didn't quite reach her eyes. Whatever he chose to do next would tell her a great deal.

"Have you heard from him? Remy, I mean. Lately?" Any effort at nonchalance was tanked by his inability—or unwillingness, she wasn't sure which, to look her in the eye when he asked.

"No. Didn't I tell you last night that when he walked out, it was the last I ever heard from him? Why are you asking me now?" EV threw the sheet off; ignored his sharp intake of breath at the sight of her naked body, and pulled her robe from its hook on her bathroom door. The sharp motion of her hands while she tied it were at odds with the utter innocence she managed to keep fixed on her face.

"No reason. I was just wondering."

"You're a lousy liar. I hope you don't play poker with that face. You'd lose your shirt. Tell me what's going on."

"Nothing." Pants. Definitely not the time to climb back into bed. He found them, pulled them over his hips. Trying to lie to EV left him feeling naked; he couldn't do it while literally undressed.

"Don't lie to me. After everything I told you last night, you have to know that's the last thing I'll tolerate. So tell me the truth, Dalton, or you need to leave."

He opened his mouth to protest, then thought

better of it. Anything he said now was likely to get him into trouble—if not with her, with Nate. He liked his job. He intended to keep it. Nate had verified that Remy Vincent was involved in blackmailing Evan Plunkett—something EV was bound to take hard. Worse, there was no way of knowing whether Vincent was finished or if he would continue to plague Ponderosa Pines. Cold fury settled in his heart; for both EV's pain and that caused to the town.

"I have to go to work. Can we talk about this later? Over dinner at my place?"

"Sorry, I have plans."

"What plans?"

"You tell me what you're hiding; I'll tell you my plans."

Dalton yanked on his boots; left them untied, and with a last frustrated look in her direction, turned and walked out of the room—and out of the house.

Chapter 22

Chloe sat on EV's living room floor, a pile of Amazon boxes overflowing around her. After ten minutes of watching EV try to assemble the first of five wildlife cameras, Chloe snatched the instructions away and sent EV into the kitchen to make a pot of coffee. By the time she returned, Chloe was working on camera number two.

EV rolled her eyes skyward and asked, "How do you do that?"

"Do what?"

"Manage to be good at everything the first time you try it."

Chloe grinned. "This isn't my first time. I took a few photography classes in college, and worked as a photographer's assistant for about six months. Damn good money for a starving student, and I learned a lot. I've gotten out of the habit of taking pictures, though."

"That's at least the tenth job I've heard you mention. What gives?"

"None of the jobs I worked felt like something I could do every day for the rest of my life. I always felt restless. Until now." Every day in Ponderosa Pines was a different experience. It satisfied Chloe's need for variety, as well as her need for a stable environment.

"I'm glad you're so happy here. And that you're staying. Wouldn't be the same without you. Now let's head out and place these contraptions." As usual, EV didn't dwell on the warm and fuzzy for long. She'd said her piece, and now it was back to business. It didn't fool Chloe; she knew how much EV cared for her, and the feeling was mutual. But she did know enough not to draw attention to the fact.

"You've been quiet since yesterday morning when I saw Dalton sneak out your back door with his boots in his hands."

"There's not much to say on the topic," EV admitted.

No snarky comment about being nosy; no quick grin; nothing more than a very subdued EV. Chloe was worried.

"Did he spend the night? Did you tell him about the baby?"

"Yes and yes."

"So what happened? How did he take the news?"

EV looked away. "He yelled at me."

"He what?" A Chloe-rant was already forming; an acid-dripping, butt-scorching, bully-busting, how-dare-you treatise on how not to kick someone when they were already down.

"For not telling anyone, for keeping it to myself all these years."

Well, Chloe thought as the rant fizzled like a spent sparkler, *I agree with him on that score.*

"He was probably right." EV acknowledged. "One thing led to another and he ended up spending the night."

"Isn't that a good thing? You're moving forward." Chloe shoved three of the cameras into her largest hiking pack. "You opened up. That's good."

"You'd think." Wry and dry. Classic EV. "In the morning, his phone rang—Nate, I think—and then he had the nerve to ask me if I'd seen Remy lately."

"Odd," Chloe frowned, "Wait. You don't think... no. But it does make sense." Even though Chloe wasn't speaking in complete sentences, EV could tell their minds ran along the same track.

"You're thinking that Dalton suspects Remy of being involved in the blackmail scheme." EV fitted two cameras into her own pack.

"Sure I am. Aren't you?"

"Dalton refused to confirm my suspicions." There was more to the story, Chloe could tell.

"What happened next?."

"He asked me to dinner, I told him I had plans."

"You don't have plans."

"It was the second time he's brought up Remy's name in the middle of a conversation about something else. Either he's stupidly jealous over someone I've not seen or heard from for thirty years, or he's hiding something. I suspected the latter and told him I have plans until he comes clean. Cue the sneaking out with his boots thing."

"Then what?"

"Then nothing. He left and that's that." When Chloe opened her mouth to ask another question, EV knew exactly how to put an end to the conversation, "The sex was surprisingly inventive. You'd never know it to look at him but Dalton has a..."

"Stop right there. Nope, I do not want to hear any

more." Horrified at what she thought EV was about to say, Chloe slapped both hands over her ears. "Not another word."

Laughing, EV picked up her pack and headed out the door.

Mounting a stealth operation to hide cameras in the woods while wearing the blaze orange that kept them from becoming another sad hunting statistic didn't exactly lend a layer of secrecy to the plan.

"Okay, that's the last of them," Chloe slid the fifth wildlife camera into place. While she gathered up the tools, EV programmed the night vision and motion detector settings. If anything passed by here in the darkness, the camera would shoot a series of images, hopefully capturing a usable shot of the town bandit.

Using simple logic, EV had picked this spot near the edge of the woods between Mr. Zellner's back field and Lottie's side yard. Both had seen something disappear, and neither had received anything in return. If the Yeti was systematically working his way back around to everyone he had stolen from, it was likely he'd hit one of their properties next. And now, with luck, they might catch an identifying shot of him. The odds were fifty-fifty for him showing up there, but that was better than nothing.

Stepping back a few feet, the two women surveyed their handiwork. With its camouflage design, the plastic housing made the cameras difficult to see even in daytime when you knew exactly where to look. Night would completely hide them.

Unless he was somewhere watching them now, the Ponderosa Pines Prowler should have no idea he was about to become a Kodak moment.

Despite the generosity of spirit normally fostered in this town, residents were calling for action. Nate and Dalton split stakeout duty between them, which only covered one location each night. So far, neither had been in the right place at the right time. Fingerprint analysis on the returned items yielded no clues. While those instant database searches on TV were no longer pure fiction, if someone had never committed a crime, their fingerprints probably were not in the system.

Given the lack of results, Nate concluded the miscreant was not a habitual offender. Items being returned supported his theory. What kind of thief returns to the scene of the crime with gifts? With the initial furor dying down, the town was beginning to realize they probably weren't in any physical danger.

Still, bringing a stop to the whole business was a priority.

Nate would not approve, though, of this particular sting operation. Chloe knew it, and so did EV, which was why they had waited until they knew he was out of town for the day before mounting the cameras. A total relief for Chloe, since it gave her a day of normalcy. Watching for him, ducking into dark corners, and avoiding places he frequented had become second nature by now. A break in that routine was welcome.

Halfway back to the truck, EV stopped abruptly enough that Chloe nearly bowled her over. "What the…" she started to ask before being shushed.

"Someone's coming." EV glanced around quickly, spotted a good hiding place, and pulled Chloe behind a cluster of large rocks deposited by glaciers on their last trip through these woods.

Voices punctuated the sound of rustling leaves and bodies crashing through bushes. "You think we're dealing with some kind of hybrid here? Can a Yeti and a Sasquatch, you know, procreate?"

"Probably, they're both furry."

"What's that got to do with anything?"

"I don't know. You're the expert on the Bigfeet."

"Bigfoot is the name of a known Sasquatch, not a technical term."

"Well, whatever, man. Jeez, don't have a cow."

Two or three Yeti hunters—Chloe guessed—judging by the amount of snapping twigs she could hear. Curious at what they might say, she and EV listened.

"Bite me. You're only here for the thrills."

"Thrills? Slogging through the woods looking for tufts of hair, or fur? Whatever."

"You don't want to stick around, you're welcome to leave."

"Nah, I'm staying. Do you think the locals would notice if we brought in a few more warm bodies? Dubicki's talking about blocking off some of these trails. He thinks he can force the 'squatch out into the open by cutting off all the escape routes."

The voices faded into the distance when the pair of young Sasq-Watchers moved on.

"We'll just see about that." EV intoned darkly.

"Bet your ass." Chloe agreed.

Chapter 23

Basil Fundy, First Selectman of Ponderosa Pines, surveyed his kitchen table with dismay. Ever since it had become obvious these thefts were an ongoing thing, it seemed to him that half the town had found some flimsy pretext to stop by his place.

On the upside, some of the visitors assumed that plying him with baked goods was the best way to spur him on to action. An apple crisp, a couple pies, two loaves of pumpkin bread, and a half dozen zucchini muffins ranged across his kitchen table. On the downside, though, Priscilla had dropped off something he couldn't quite identify.

At first glance, it kind of looked like cake—if there was such a thing as cake that came in this unappetizing gray color. No such confection came to mind, which suggested it was probably something else. Meat? Yes, he decided it was probably meatloaf, but after peeling back the plastic for a sniff test, he couldn't swear to it. Whatever it was, it smelled of nothing he could immediately identify. At that point, his brain suggested the absolute worst possibility.

Tofu loaf.

When EV called with the latest, Basil decided he'd better initiate an emergency town meeting to discuss the best way of running those Sasq-Watcher folks out of town. After that, it was a matter of activating the phone tree. Beginning with his second in command, who suggested a two-day delay and the addition of a potluck supper to help relieve tension, Basil set the ball in motion.

Seconding the potluck idea, Basil knew exactly what he would contribute to the potluck supper. An apple pie, a loaf of pumpkin bread, and Priscilla's mystery dish.

Basil rapped his gavel against the small wooden sounding block that lay in readiness at the corner of his customary spot at the table in front of the room. Now that his poker night plans had gone down in a flaming ball of wreckage, he might as well get this gripe session underway. Besides, Nate Harper and Dalton Burnsoll were the ones most likely taking heat tonight. After weeks of systematic pilfering, the local gumshoes were no closer to finding the culprit than they had been on the first day. Worse, that band of Yeti hunters was settling in for the long haul.

The bang of the gavel echoed off the hard surfaces of the town hall meeting space. At one end, a raised stage—accessed by a small staircase on either side—served as a platform for school plays, dances, and pageants. Every third Friday night during the winter, the entertainment committee cleared the large room to make space for roller skating parties.

"Can't we do something? They're not obeying the posted signs. My best milk cow is so spooked she doesn't want to leave the barn." Tank Daniels twisted an old ball cap in hands chapped from working in the chill of morning.

"They knocked down a patch of sunflowers I hadn't gotten a chance to cut the heads off of yet. If that wasn't enough, they put up a portable duck blind in my back field without asking permission. I'm pretty sure they've taken pictures of me without permission." Zellner shouted. "Besides, everyone knows all Yetis live on Mount Everest. Even if they migrated, they're not coming below the snow line. Can't tell the difference between a Sasquatch and a Yeti, they ought not be allowed out in public alone."

Zellner's tirade spurred Nate to action before he had time to devote more than a passing thought to Mr. Zellner's possible closet enthusiast status. After all, he did know a little too much detail about the difference between a Yeti and a Sasquatch. Nate strode to the front of the room to address the crowd. "There's no Yeti in our woods," he directed a stern look at Mr. Zellner, "And no Sasquatch, either."

From the back of the room, a voice rose above the mutter of agreement from the crowd. "I think it's like one of those Christmas movies where Santa Claus crashes his sleigh during a trial run and gets amnesia. That's why he's bringing back the things he stole. Or wait, was that the Grinch?"

Nate held up a hand. "It's not Santa; and, I can promise you, it's not the Grinch." He kept his gaze away from where Chloe sat adjacent to EV. One glance at the smirk he knew was already on her face, and he'd be done. Not that she would spare him a look anyway.

"The Grinch is a fictional character." Scorn dripped from Zellner's voice like poison from a viper's tongue. A snort issued from the side of the room Nate had been studiously ignoring, and he had to bite the inside of his lip to keep from busting out one of his own. He noticed Zellner left the option open for there still being a Santa Claus.

Only in Ponderosa Pines would he have the option to engage in a public debate over the fictional status of Bigfoot versus The Grinch. God, he loved this place.

And that's when he decided he was staying. Chloe or no Chloe. This was home. These were his people, for better or for worse—caring folks who were always willing to look for the good in people. Okay, maybe not in the Yeti hunters.

The decision made, Nate worked to hold back the grin that wanted to curl the corners of his mouth. The last thing he wanted to do was invite more grief into his life by letting Mr. Zellner think Nate found his opinion laugh-worthy.

"Can we agree that the thief is not Bigfoot? Or a fictional character?" Nate waited to see if anyone else wanted to become the voice of dissent. No takers. At least he had that going for him.

"And can we also agree that this crew of Sasquatch seekers needs to go?" A roar of agreement rose from the crowd.

"Can't you just tell them to leave?" Horis questioned.

Nate sighed. He wished it were that easy. "Technically, they're not doing anything wrong. I'll have a word with them about the trespassing— and yes, EV, about them blocking trails." She settled back in her chair. "But if they don't break any laws, I can't just run them out of town. The best I can do is prove that he's not a Sasquatch, and hope they decide to move on."

"Isn't that your job?" This from Priscilla Lewellyn, who loved nothing more than to throw another log on the fire.

Dalton, who had remained seated at Nate's side, rose and responded, "You know we don't exactly have the largest police force, and these woods cover a lot of ground. We've been canvassing during the day, and staking out different spots each night. We'll catch this fellow, don't you worry about that."

"You had better, Burnsoll, or some of us are ready to take matters into our own hands." Tank's words rung out. Basil's gavel interrupted the response that had been poised on Nate's tongue.

"We will not resort to vigilante justice; we can't have word getting out that Ponderosa Pines doesn't welcome tourists. Like it or not, our occasional guests make up a portion of our town revenue. Give Harper and Burnsoll a chance; we'll reconvene if the problem isn't solved in a timely manner."

Nate chanced a glance at Chloe, who had been studying his face through lowered lashes ever since the Tank Daniels threat. For a fleeting moment, their eyes met, and the rest of the room faded away. That was when the meeting ended, and as people started rising from their chairs the spell was broken. When the crowd cleared, Chloe was gone.

Chapter 24

Dalton zipped up his fanny pack—or, as his ex-wife used to call it, his dork sack—and pulled his hunter's orange sweatshirt down to cover it up. Stylish or not, the fanny pack was a useful hiking accessory, and he refused to stop wearing it. What difference did it make now, anyway? He didn't have anyone to impress; EV was the one, and since they were at odds yet again, it didn't matter.

He needed fresh air, and some peace and quiet. A nice hike along his favorite trail seemed like a perfect way to clear his head. Duty kept him from giving her the details he and Nate had turned up on Vincent, but that same duty was keeping them apart. Her ability to sense that he was holding something back put them at odds—and right when she'd finally let him in. Now all he could think about was how her skin felt under his hands; how she had tasted, smelled; how much he wanted her again.

Straight ahead, Dalton could see someone standing at the edge of the boat dock, looking out at the lake. Moving closer, he realized it was Chloe. Her hunched posture alone was enough to tell him she was hurting over something. "Hi there." She rubbed a hand across her face, cleared her throat, and looked up into his eyes. Dalton realized she had been crying, but the determined set of her jaw dissuaded him from asking any questions.

"Hi, Dalton. What are you up to?"

"Oh, I'm hiking my pain away. You?" he ventured.

Chloe's eyes focused on something in the middle of the pond. "The same." She said simply.

"I know we don't know each other all that well, but if you want to talk about it, I'm game." His gentle smile tugged at Chloe's heartstrings. Everything she knew about him told her he was trustworthy; he wouldn't go back and blab all her secrets to Nate. So instead of holding back, as she normally would, Chloe let loose a deluge of frustration that neither she, nor Dalton, had expected.

"I'm angry at your stupid partner. Everyone keeps saying he's in love with me, but apparently, he's not;

I've seen his hot, redheaded girlfriend around a couple of times. I knew I shouldn't have let myself have feelings for him. I knew I'd just get hurt and ruin our friendship. He shouldn't have flirted with me if he wasn't interested. Or maybe I imagined the flirting. Hell, it's been quite a while since I've had a relationship, or even a crush for that matter. I'm probably acting like a teenager. But I'm still mad." She finished petulantly.

When Dalton didn't say anything in response, Chloe suddenly felt as though she had made a mistake. "Look, I'm sorry. I shouldn't have said anything. I didn't mean to put you in an awkward position. I'll see you around." She turned to walk away, but Dalton placed a hand on her arm.

"No, Chloe, that's not it. Stay and talk. Are you really serious about Nate? Are you in love with him?"

Chloe considered the question. "I've been trying to answer that question myself ever since he came back to town. It hasn't ever been easy for me to get attached to anyone; I learned not to, after being uprooted so many times as a kid. The people here, in the Pines, always felt permanent—even though I only saw them occasionally. When he first came home, I thought we would fall back into the friend routine. But after seeing him with that *woman*, I realized that I've probably always been fooling myself. When you don't know what you're missing, it can be hard to recognize it when it pops up in front of your face."

"Well, that's certainly true."

"Don't get me wrong: I didn't have some horrible childhood. I was always taken care of; I was always loved. There are so many benefits to the lifestyle I was given, but the grass is always greener on the other side. I experienced so many wonderful things in this world, and now I want to experience the wonderful things about settling down and being in a committed, loving relationship." Chloe couldn't believe what she was about to say out loud, to Dalton, of all people.

"Yes, I'm in love with Nate. It's not just about stuffing some hole in my heart with whatever I can cram in there. It's about the fact that I didn't realize how deep the hole was... until he filled it. And now he's there, but not really."

"So why don't you tell him? It seems like the kind of thing a guy would like to hear" He spoke from experience.

"I've been saying it's because I think he'll leave;

go back to Portland and I'll be left alone again. I don't want to live anywhere but here, and he wants to live anywhere else. Though, I will admit that it's more about being scared of getting hurt."

"Well, what I can tell you is that keeping yourself closed off is going to hurt you for sure. You may or may not get hurt by opening up, but you can be damned sure that denying your feelings is a recipe for disaster. I can also tell you that Nate doesn't hate the Pines. I think he might already have decided to stay."

Chloe turned this new information over in her mind. Could Dalton be right? He'd be the one to know; he spent nearly every day with Nate. There was still one problem.

"He's already moved on. If you can move on from something that never even started, that is. And he's pulling away from me. We can't even talk without fighting anymore. Or without some kind of tension. Plus—girlfriend." She waved a hand to indicate he was forgetting the obvious.

"That tension is caused by mutual, unrequited feelings; it doesn't take a genius to see that. I'm going to tell you something, and I'm probably going to get my ass handed to me for doing so. But I can't sit around and watch you two mess up your relationship. Elise is not Nate's girlfriend. She's a private investigator he hired to help figure out who was blackmailing Evan Plunkett."

He let the revelation sink in for a moment before continuing. "He worked with her in Portland, and when the elders urged—or rather, ordered—us to put a stop to the investigation; we had to take it underground for a while. I think part of him enjoyed that she made you uncomfortable." Dalton reached down for a stone to toss into the lake. "Nate's stubborn, same as you. You two are peas from the same pod; sometimes that's not a good thing, and sometimes it is. Talk to him. Don't *Chloe-rant* at him."

"That's a term we're using now? Excellent." Chloe deadpanned, somewhat unsuccessfully. Dalton could see hope shining in her eyes. Chloe leaned over and gave Dalton a kiss on the cheek. "You're a wonderful man, Earnest Dalton Burnsoll. EV is lucky to have you in her life." She treated him to a grin, "Not as lucky as you are to have her, I'd say, but then, I'm biased."

"I don't think I do have her. Not after the way she ran me out of the house after we..." his face flamed red. Chloe barely resisted the urge to tease.

"Be patient. She's been on her own for way too

long; I truly believe you two will wind up together in the end."

"You're a sweet girl for saying so, and I hope you're right. Maybe we'll both get a happy ending."

And the urge won. "From what I heard, you already did." With a saucy grin at his flaming face, she turned, and, feeling lighter in her heart than she had in weeks, walked away down the path toward home.

Chapter 25

This time, it was Chloe who rose early—and in good spirits, to boot. It was EV who was sleepy and out of sorts. The revelation that Nate wasn't dating had calmed Chloe's ruffled nerves, and removed a significant weight from her chest. Feeling charitable, she had volunteered herself and EV to rake leaves at the church this unseasonably warm Saturday morning. Chattering away, Chloe barely noticed EV's funk.

"Do you have any of those big orange yard bags that look like pumpkins left? I was thinking we could decorate our backyards and do a little haunted house kind of thing for the kids. Wouldn't that be fun? I'm really getting into the holiday spirit this year, and I think the weather is going to hold out, so it won't be completely frigid for trick-or-treating. Let's make popcorn balls, and caramel apples!"

Chloe's enthusiasm was infectious, and by the

time they had accumulated three full bags of leaves, EV had suggested asking Horis to dress up as a zombie farmer for their more-spectacular-by-the-second Halloween party.

Across the churchyard, a white shape caught EV's eye. She pointed and called to Chloe, "Look over there. Is that white thing moving? I don't have my glasses…"

Chloe squinted, and after a second, a grin spread across her face. "It's that little rascal, Drambuie. Let's go." EV grabbed Chloe's rake from her hands and leaned both it and her own up against the side of the church.

"We need to go slow, or we'll scare him." EV headed for the edge of the woods, curling around the border where the cat was standing. Chloe fell in behind her, moving as quickly and quietly as possible through the fallen layer of leaves and pine needles.

They were close, and getting closer, when the cat turned and caught sight of them. His eyes bugged out, his tail shot straight up right before he spun and bolted toward the woods. EV took off after him, snaking through the trees with the ease and swift-ness of a woman half her age. Chloe followed, and for a full five minutes ran, zigzagging across fallen trees and around walls of thick brush. Drambuie, being smaller and far more agile, disappeared over the crest of a hill. By the time Chloe and EV were able to catch up, he was long gone.

EV bent over, placing her hands on her knees to catch her breath. "Well, that was a nice workout. At least we can tell Lottie he's still alive, and apparently, thriving."

"While we're out here, we might as well collect the memory cards from the wildlife cameras. It shouldn't take too long."

"Let's do it. I was tired of raking leaves, anyway." Covering the remaining distance at a much slower pace allowed time and energy for conversation. "We've been so caught up in this business with the thefts and the Sasquatch hunters; we haven't had any time to work on solving the blackmailer mystery."

"Oh, I haven't told you yet. I talked to Dalton yesterday." Chloe paused, chancing a glance at her friend. Dalton was a touchy subject, and Chloe did not want to risk poking the bear.

"Go on."

"He told me that Nate's not dating Elise. She's a private investigator he hired to try and identify the blackmailer. Apparently, he's been working the case this whole time, but the elders told him to stay out of it. So he had to keep it quiet." Chloe blurted, in a rush that wasn't quite quick enough to distract EV from the most important part of the revelation.

"That's why you're so damned peppy today. You found out Inspector Hottie *is* still on the market! I knew something was up with you; you barely even sipped your coffee, and you haven't snapped at me once." EV teased, knowing full well she'd get a rise out of her friend.

"Go eat worms." Chloe stomped off, but didn't get far before EV's long gait caught up to her. "Chloe and Nate, sittin' in a tree..."

Chapter 26

"Ready?" Chloe asked EV as she pulled the memory card out of the fourth digital camera and slipped it into a port on her laptop. All irritation at EV's insistent prodding about her relationship with Nate was long forgotten.

"Less than I was when we were checking camera number one. We're down to two memory cards left to look at, and so far—bupkus. Cross your fingers." Seconds later, another slide show of night-vision images appeared on the screen.

The first three photos featured a marauding skunk: a small, hunched over animal covered in black fur; the notorious white stripe up the back was a dead giveaway. Chloe flicked through several shots where, other than the trees, she could see nothing at all—probably triggered by the wind or an animal not visible in the frame. Her next click netted the first glimpse of the man who had been causing a ruckus amongst Ponderosa Pines residents over the last few weeks.

Early morning frost covered the blanket of fallen leaves along the forest floor, and bare trees provided a backdrop before which stood a tall, shaggy-looking man. In profile, an untamed beard billowed to at least an inch below his jawline; straggly hair protruded from a camouflage-print cap perched atop his head. The mystery man—for he was, indeed, a man—sported a canvas backpack that looked full to bursting, and carried a walking stick in one hand. EV and Chloe turned to one another, wide-eyed, but unable to utter a sound. Chloe took a deep breath and clicked to the next photograph.

This time, the man was staring in the direction of the camera, his line of sight positioned above and slightly to the left of the frame. From the front, even through the whiskers and dirt that caked his gaunt face, the man's expression was calm and gentle. A slightly wild, but benign, sadness showed in his eyes. "What do you suppose happened to him? I would guess he's been out in the woods for a good couple of months, considering the length of his beard and hair." EV asked, her eyes still riveted to the image.

"I couldn't begin to venture a guess." Chloe

clicked to the next photograph, and was once again taken aback, but for a completely different reason this time. The Yeti, as Chloe had begun to refer to him—and would probably continue to refer to him until his real name came to light—was crouched down, arms curled around a fuzzy ball of white fur. Drambuie had apparently found a companion; and, the Yeti had found a friend. In this shot, he was peering down at the cat, his mouth turned up in an indulgent smile as he scratched Drambuie's chin. This was no psychopath; this was a lost man who had obviously been through some sort of traumatic event.

EV was the first to speak, having collected herself sufficiently. "Well, he seems like a regular guy; which is what we've been expecting since the art attack he launched on the town."

"Now the question is: what do we do with these photos? We have to give them to Nate, obviously. But, I'm going to do some research of my own first—now that I know what he looks like, I can narrow my search." Chloe's eyes took on a faraway look, and EV knew she was already formulating a plan and making a mental list of websites to visit.

"I'll put on a kettle for tea and order some food. That bus boy at the Mudbucket delivers if I throw him a fiver. I'll go grab my laptop while we wait; then we can tackle this together. I can look through missing persons reports while you scour social media for our guy."

"Perfect." Chloe replied, settling on a cushioned dining room chair with her laptop. Within minutes, she had logged into Facebook and opened several group pages related to missing persons. When EV returned with her computer, she spent the time while it booted up puttering around making tea and tidying up Chloe's normally spotless kitchen before answering the door and paying for their food delivery.

"Thanks, Bobby. We really appreciate it. Put this towards your college fund." Bobby nodded.

"Thanks, EV." EV thought she detected an eye roll, and she would have been correct.

The two women chatted, contemplating the Yeti's true identity while they enjoyed a couple of the Mudbucket's famous veggie wraps and split a chocolate whoopie pie. Chloe kept one eye on her computer screen, occasionally reaching over to tap the scroll button and check for possible matches.

Several hours passed before EV reached her limit, stood up, and attempted to throw one of the kittens' toy mice across the dining room. It flew all of three feet before Spice sailed in from out of nowhere and pounced. He skittered sideways before picking up the toy and racing through the kitchen, feet slipping and sliding along the tile floor.

"Come look at this one." Chloe called to EV for at least the dozenth time that evening, having needed confirmation on several possible matches. EV reluctantly, and with little faith that this prospective would be the correct one, rose from her chair and walked around to stand behind Chloe and peer over her shoulder.

"Oh my Goddess, that's him! Don't you think?" She nearly did a little dance when she realized they finally had a name to go with the face. Though, the fact that Chloe had even recognized him surprised the hell out of EV. The man in the missing persons photograph was an entirely different person: incredibly fit and healthy-looking, attractive even; his face lacking the wistful sadness from the photograph they had taken.

"Christian West is his name. I can't believe it's the same man. His mother says he left about four months ago to go on an extended hiking trip on the Appalachian Trail. Six weeks later, he stopped checking in. First, his family filed a report, and when the authorities failed to turn up anything, launched an extensive search."

EV looked at the most recent updates on the efforts to find Christian West. She stood in silence for a long moment. Chloe could see the wheels turning until, comprehension dawning on her face, EV ran around to her seat at the table, and pulled up a map. "They're looking in the wrong spot; they're too far away and they don't even realize it. There's something playing at the edge of my mind. It feels like once it jogs loose, I'll know where he is."

"He's a real outdoorsy type; survivalist and whatnot. How fortunate for him to have found the Pines. Maybe it was the mothership calling him home." Chloe snorted. "Graduated from Northwestern, with honors. Art major, 'earth and planetary studies' minor. Something must have happened to him out there." Chloe had started to realize that in addition to getting rid of the Yeti hunters, they could potentially reunite a grieving family.

Without stopping to think, or ponder the consequences of her decision, Chloe shot a private message to the woman listed as Christian's mother. Not expecting an immediate answer, given the late hour,

Chloe began to scroll through the photographs on Christian's own Facebook page. All evidence so far seemed to eliminate the possibility that he was dangerous. Seconds later, an answering message came through; Mrs. West asked Chloe to call her, and left an out-of-state cell phone number. EV held her breath as Chloe made the call.

Chapter 27

"I've been an idiot," EV's voice spiked in Chloe's ear after she'd grunted a terse, "What?"

"Camp Doodlemungus."

"Camp what the whatsis? It's…" Chloe cracked one eye open. When the blur cleared, she read the clock. "5:00 am. When they list your time of death, it's going to say 5:05 on the certificate."

"Like you could haul yourself out of bed in a mere five minutes," EV scoffed.

"Why are you still talking to me? You should be getting a head start."

"Didn't you hear what I said? I know where Christian is."

"And this news couldn't wait another two hours?"

"Get dressed; we're going on a hike."

"Call Nate. Let him deal with it. I'm going back to sleep."

"I already did. He and Dalton are on their way over. I talked him into letting us tag along."

"Talked him into it?"

"Okay, I railroaded him. Happy?. I refused to give him the name you found, and told him we were going whether he liked it or not. And that I know a short-cut, so we'd probably get there first. He caved pretty quickly. Don't you want to go?"

Did she? Maybe it was time to confront her issues with Nate head on.

Shuddering, she remembered her last attempt to avoid contact with the bane of her existence. She had just walked out of Thread with a bag of specially-ordered cashmere yarn—Veronica was getting a sweater for Christmas—when he rounded the corner. Absorbed in a phone conversation, he hadn't noticed her immediately, so Chloe had dodged across the narrow sidewalk to duck in front of Horis' truck where it was parked out front. She assumed the truck's owner was grabbing a sandwich from The Mudbucket.

From her place of concealment, she heard Nate's footsteps. Staying crouched; she sidled along the outside of the truck, but couldn't quite resist a peek. When Chloe lifted her head to peer through the bottom of the truck's side window, it was with great surprise that she found herself looking right into Horis' amused face. Apparently, he'd had a front row seat for her entire stealth operation.

Chloe's face burned again when she remembered how she had held a finger to her lips, and begged with her eyes to keep Horis from telling what he'd seen. Still, the man was a sweetheart. Without missing a beat, he'd crossed his heart, and then repeated her finger-to-lips gesture.

"That won't be awkward." She wasn't awake enough to give the statement the eye roll it deserved. "And we couldn't do this after the freaking sun comes up?"

"Haul your lazy ass out of bed and be here in fifteen." EV hung up while Chloe fumed.

"Who does she think she is?" Chloe demanded of Sugar who, wakened by all the commotion, had crawled up onto Chloe's chest for a cuddle and a purr.

She was still holding her phone when she heard the soft beep of an incoming text message.

Wear layers, it's chilly out.

Bite me. I'm not coming.

Quit complaining. Don't you know it's Daylight Savings Time, your body thinks it's 6:00 am.

You are pure evil, and I'm not coming.

Right. See you in a few minutes.

There were two things Chloe knew; if EV had given her fifteen minutes, she really had twenty; and she was going to climb out of bed and get dressed, because her curiosity would not let her go back to sleep.

Fifteen minutes or twenty made no difference; neither gave her time enough to take a shower. With a quick, ruthless series of movements, she yanked her hair back into a tail which she threaded through the back of an old ball cap.

Spice watched the action with great interest. Kill The Pony Tail was one of her favorite games. She gathered herself to leap, but Chloe warned the kitten off by speaking her name in a low tone.

Pouring on the speed, she applied just enough makeup to look more awake than she really felt, fed the cats, and bustled out the door into the burgeoning light of dawn.

EV expected to spend the day walking on eggshells, or maybe hot coals. Chloe was mad at

Nate; Nate was annoyed with Chloe; Dalton was high on EV's list of people to avoid—and she'd bet she rated right up there on his. Judging by Nate's clipped tones, he hadn't been happy to have the case solved for him.

Oh goody.

She'd given Chloe fifteen minutes, knowing she'd take at least twenty, and that would give them ten to prepare themselves before the men arrived.

"I hate you." By now, the grumpiness was all for show. The idea of getting one up on Nate had blown away most of the morning cobwebs. The to-go cup of coffee EV handed her would brush way the rest.

"Where is this Camp Googlyfungus?"

"Doodlemungus."

"Whatever." Second thoughts about spending too much time with Nate surfaced about the time Chloe stepped through EV's front door. "Stupid name, anyway."

"Hey, your mother was a Greenie in the Eco Scouts."

EV grinned when Chloe's eyes rounded in surprise.

Chloe giggled. "Nice Yo Mama comeback, but they're not supposed to be true, you know."

"If memory serves, she was the one to name the camp." EV ratted Lila out without a second thought.

"That almost makes up for you dragging me out of dreamland to go on the hike from hell. Why didn't we wait and go alone later to scope it out?"

"I promised Dalton I would call him before I did anything dangerous."

"Wait, do you think this might be dangerous?"

EV shook her head. "No, not at all."

"I see. So, you're annoying me while trying to score brownie points with Dalton?" It was close enough to the truth that EV shot Chloe a quelling look before saying, "It's a win-win. Look at the evidence. He stole things; he repaired those things, and then he returned them. That's not someone who intends to do harm. Besides, you saw him cuddling Drambuie in the photo. He's not dangerous."

Chloe agreed. Since the first phone call, a flurry of private messages had buzzed across the net between Chloe and Christian's mother. Mrs. West explained the series of events leading to her son's decision to hike the Appalachian Trail.

Her description of how Christian, on his way home from work, had come upon a house fire. He'd called 9-1-1, and then, when a frantic woman ran out of the house screaming that her babies were trapped inside, Christian took action.

With no thought for his own safety, he had run into the burning building. The smoke filled his lungs; burned his eyes, but still, he managed to find the nursery where a small bundle wrapped in a pink blanket lay much too still in the crib. Choking, he'd grabbed the baby, turned to leave when he heard the thin cries of another small child. Quickly, Christian had detoured into the next room. Fire roared on the other side of the wall; there wasn't much time. Precious seconds passed while he searched the room with watering eyes while he choked on the thick, black fumes. Finally, he spotted a sneakered foot poking out from under the bed, grabbed the ankle, and pulled.

Shouting that he was there to help, he hoisted the little boy in his free arm and raced outside to collapse, gasping, on the grass.

The little boy survived; the baby didn't make it.

Christian blamed himself. In the year that followed, he began to exhibit symptoms of PTSD.

It started with nightmares, the kind that pulled him screaming out of bed. Every night he got less sleep than the night before. His once-cheerful face fell into lines of stress; he forgot how to smile. When the flashbacks started, he gave in and sought help.

After several months of therapy, his mother said he'd been in recovery; that he intended to use this hiking trip as a sort of renaissance period. It had been going well until he missed one of his regular check-ins, then another. Given his history, the authorities feared the worst but his folks still hoped for the best.

Now he was several weeks missing, and everyone assumed he was much farther south than where the trail ran adjacent to Ponderosa Pines.

Christian's mother painted a clear picture of a man who had had his fair share of troubles, but was working at rising above them before his disappearance.

All of this Chloe explained to Dalton, while not risking so much as a glance at Nate. Her attempt to dispel the awkwardness only half worked, but it took up the first five minutes of the hike.

Nate had spoken only two words. "Let's go," before he gestured for EV to lead the way. Chloe wanted to tell him he'd make better time if he pulled that stick out of his butt. She took the high road, knowing it wouldn't earn her any points. Instead, she walked behind him and imagined darts shooting out of her eyes.

Dalton brought up the rear, which ensured he wouldn't have to say anything to EV, while EV's long legs ate up the ground. Chloe glanced over her shoulder to see Dalton's gaze pinned on EV's back. What a bunch of idiots they all were. Every last one of them. Not that she planned on breaking the ice with Nate.

After ten minutes, though, the silence crept in on her like spiders through a crack in a wall; its fingers nearly as shivery on her neck as one of their hairy legs would have been. She couldn't stand it.

"Don't we at least get credit for calling you this time—you know, before we just went ahead and did something without you?" She tossed the question over her shoulder toward Dalton.

He shrugged.

She turned again; glared at Dalton until a tiny smile played around his lips. Though, that might have been because he saw the root she was about to trip over right before her foot snagged it. Her short cry triggered Nate's quick reflexes. He spun and caught her in time to stop her from doing a total face plant.

Flames ignited where he touched her; inched up to color her face red as Chloe stammered, "Thank you."

As soon as she was solidly on her feet again, Nate snatched his hands back as if the flames she felt had also burned his skin. For the first time all day, EV and Dalton's eyes met. The two shared a smile over the fumbling of the young and in love.

Something else passed between them; the knowledge that the boat they were in was very similar. Okay, maybe a lot older and a bit more decrepit, but not so very different. EV jammed her hands into her pockets and deadpanned, "We're getting close to Camp. Maybe you have a trumpet you'd like to blow. You know—so you can announce our presence with as much fanfare as possible. I'm not sure all the yelling is enough."

Nate positioned a hand above the butt of his gun, but EV gestured to him with impatience. "For Pete's sake, you idiot. You're not going into an ambush with an armed robbery suspect. Relax."

"You don't know what he's capable of," Nate cautioned.

"I know he's capable of running into a burning building to save a stranger's children."

Nate dropped his hand away from the gun, but remained tense—ready for anything.

Not that he could have prepared himself for his first view of Camp Doodlemungus.

Christian sat in an old camp chair—one EV recognized from her days as an Eco Scout—feet outstretched toward an open fire enclosed by a circle of stones, his hands busily worked a small jackknife over a piece of ash. Tears ran down the man's face as the form of a smiling baby took shape under his skill, and the sharp blade of the knife.

He heard them coming; couldn't have helped it since they made no real effort at stealth.

"Figured you'd find me eventually." His voice sounded rough from disuse and emotion.

"You're Christian West." Nate pulled his jacket back to reveal the badge clipped to his belt. "Detective Nate Harper." His action also revealed the gun holster.

"Yes, sir." Christian laid down his knife. Slowly he raised both hands. "I'm unarmed, and I won't fight you. I swear it."

"Don't be ridiculous. We're not here to arrest you." When Nate exaggeratedly cleared his throat, EV glared at him. "Keep quiet, Harper." She turned back to Christian, "I'm EV Torrence, this is Chloe LaRue, and that's Dalton Burnsoll. We're the official Ponderosa Pines welcoming committee."

Nate didn't even try to hide a snort.

Ignoring him, EV spoke again to Christian, "Your family has been worried sick about you, young man. Would you like to tell us what happened?" She reached into the small pack she carried to retrieve the thermos of hot chocolate and the thick BLT sandwich she'd put together before leaving this morning.

Christian accepted the food gratefully.

"Call me Chris."

"Chris." EV crouched beside the chair to lay a hand on his arm; infused her voice with sympathy. "Please tell us what happened to you."

The young man looked at each of the four of them in turn. He reached up to pull the ball cap from his head, brushed back the wild tangles of dirty hair to show a healing contusion at his temple.

"I'll tell you what I can, but my memory is a little sketchy. I was hiking north with just three more days to go before I'd come out to where Trail Buddies left my pickup." He glanced around, "You know about Trail Buddies? For a small fee, you can leave your vehicle with them and they'll drop you off wherever you want to start hiking. Then on the day before you plan to finish, they deliver your vehicle to the exit point and lock it up with the keys in it. I sure hope it's still there."

"Finish your story, then I'll put in a call to have someone check on it for you," Nate reassured him.

"Thanks. I really do appreciate that." Christian fell silent until EV reminded him that he was telling them his story. The short hesitation made her think he might still be suffering the effects of the blow to his head.

"Oh, right. Well, it was stupid really, I saw a break in the trees up on the top of a hill, and figured the view with the autumn leaves would be photo-worthy. I had to climb up on a boulder, but it was spectacular. I took a few—maybe half a dozen shots before I fell. Lost my phone, I guess, since I don't seem to have it anymore."

"When your family reported you missing, state police tried to access your phone's GPS. They found it almost ten miles southwest of here, which is why the search radius was centered in the wrong place all this time. What else do you remember?"

"Nasty headache, a lot of walking. By the time I found this place, I was in rough shape. Cold, hungry, in pain. I barely remember finding this little cabin in the woods. There were a few packs of freeze-dried camping meals in an old metal tin, and that held me for a little while. I slept a lot, and each time I woke up, my thinking was a little clearer."

"Looks like you took a hard one to the temple." Dalton finally spoke.

"Scrambled my eggs." Christian smiled. "I'm not sure how many days I'd been here before I found the little town." Now his gaze fell. "I stole food from the fields, from outside one of the buildings, and milk from somebody's cows."

"That would be Tank." Chloe interjected. "It's okay," she said, when she saw his stricken expression. "He's a good man who doesn't hold a grudge. But, why didn't you come on into town and ask for help?"

It was the question they all wanted to hear answered.

Christian dropped his face into his hands. "You've talked to my mother?"

"Yes, I have." Chloe injected as much warmth and understanding as she could into her tone. His story had touched her deeply.

"Ever since the...ever since, I've had trouble

asking for help. So I stole what I needed. But, eventually, my conscience started poking at me, so I looked for a way to give something back."

"And that's when you took the broken items and fixed them."

"I've always liked working with my hands. When I saw that box of art supplies, I knew it was wrong, but I took it. I used the paints; made my own glue and resins. There's no excusing what I did. I know you have to take me to jail. Could you please make sure my mom gets this to where it should go?" He handed EV the carving of the baby.

The look EV aimed at Nate promised death with a sharp object if he so much as reached for a set of cuffs before she assured Christian, "I think you'll be able to do that yourself. The good people of Ponderosa Pines are not vindictive enough to punish someone who needed help."

Chapter 28

While the Wests were piling into Nate's car outside the Portland Jetport and racing Ponderosa Pines to see their son for the first time in several months, Christian was enjoying a long and much-needed shower at Chloe's house. EV puttered around the kitchen making lunch for everyone. She'd already plugged into the grapevine to send two texts. One to convene a meeting of town members only; the other to arrange a distraction that would take the Sasq-Watchers out of play for the day.

"Do you think he's alright?" Chloe asked EV. "The shower shut off a while ago. I'm going to check on him."

"Christian?" she asked, as she tapped lightly at the door. "Are you okay?"

The bathroom door opened, and when Christian emerged with an exuberant smile on his face, Chloe knew he would make it through just fine. Unable to hold back a matching grin, she led him to a place at her dining room table and watched Christian inhale two sandwiches, a bowl of chowder, and a heaping portion of leftover blueberry cobbler EV had found in her refrigerator.

He was licking the last forkful clean when Chloe heard a rap on the front door. She figured Dalton must have been leading the way, because Nate never bothered knocking at all. "Are you ready?" she directed at Christian, whose eyes were like saucers in anticipation. A woman's voice wafted through the entryway. Christian remained rooted to the floor, unable to move, until his mother rounded the corner and nearly tackled him in a tearful hug. Mr. West strode over to his wife and son, wrapping his arms around them both.

Chloe and EV exchanged glances; moved to join Nate and Dalton, who had retired to the living room in order to give the Wests some privacy. Before they could make it across the kitchen, Mrs. West stepped out of the embrace. "I don't know how to thank you. I...we...you have no idea what we've been going through." She trailed off, choked by emotion and gratitude.

The room erupted into a flurry of hugs, handshakes, and heartfelt thanks; Nate and Dalton, who had been eavesdropping from the living room, eased around the corner and into the kitchen to participate. Romantic issues would have to take a backseat; there were more important things happening right now.

Christian, his eyes bright red and shining, addressed the group with more poise and confidence than she had yet to see from him. "It's me who needs to thank all of you. I hope I can find some way to repay you for your kindness."

"You don't owe us anything. That's not how it works here in the Pines." EV assured him. "Though, come to think of it, maybe there is a way you can help us."

To the consternation of Mr. Zellner, who sputtered and fumed, but eventually agreed with the rest, no one would be pressing charges against Christian.

"I'm not in favor of kicking a man when he's down, but shouldn't he at least do some community service?" Zellner insisted. "He never gave me anything for payment when he stole the clothes right off my scarecrow's back. And that wire never turned up again, either."

Lottie stood to defend Christian. He had cleaned

up a fine looking young man. Not old enough for her, to her everlasting regret. "You would have given him those items if he had asked."

"Well, he didn't. So we'll never know, now will we?"

Before Lottie could argue her point, Christian rose, held a hand up to stop her, and then turned to offer, "Mr. Zellner, if there's a bed for me somewhere here, I'd like to make it up to you by helping with whatever work you might have around your place." He'd caught the Ponderosa Pines bug, and wanted to stay.

"I guess that would be okay." Nonplussed, Zellner capitulated. He could use an able-bodied helper to finish buttoning up for the winter. "I have a spare room. You could probably stay there." the old man muttered. "You don't snore do you?"

A mile wide grin. "Not that I know of."

With that settled, the next order of business was ridding the town of its current scourge: The Sasq-Watchers.

The method for dealing with them could have been handled in many different ways; chief among them, simply revealing Christian's story to Dubicki and his nuisance of a crew. That would have been easy, safe, and effective. The downside was that it would have exposed Christian to the media. And it wouldn't have been nearly as much fun.

Instead, residents of Ponderosa Pines turned to what they did best: getting creative.

"I have an idea," EV stated with a wicked grin. And then, she laid out a simple, but brilliant, plan.

With the town on board, it took four days to get everything ready.

Everyone played a part except for Sabra Pruitt. Tied up with the hunters, she had yet to meet Christian, and was still obsessed with the Sasquatch theory. An unwitting beard, Sabra spent those four days on one fruitless search after another. It wasn't difficult to deflect their efforts away from town. A little gossip dropped at the right time and place was enough to send Sabra scurrying back to their base camp with a tall tale about a possible sighting. EV felt no remorse whatsoever for using Sabra. This whole debacle was her fault, anyway.

Stage one, EV and Chloe volunteered for a trip to an outdoor chain store in Warren, where they planned to clean the place out of its stock of Ghillie suits. Meant to provide camouflage, the shaggy suits were made from some lightweight, stringy material that was supposed to resemble moss or dead grass. With a little color alteration—instant Sasquatch. Or, more precisely, instant army of Sasquatches.

"You think these eight will be enough?" Chloe began tossing Ghillie suits into the shopping cart.

"I think so. And the breakaway props?" The list in EV's head distracted her. She repeated it over and over at the oddest times.

"I told you, Overnight shipping, they'll be here tomorrow. Relax, we're all set." Her eyes widened as Chloe pointed to a mannequin dressed in a white Ghillie, "Look, it's the latest in Yeti couture."

"Zellner would love this. It's the abominable snowman."

"I'm buying one." Chloe found a size small, and tossed it into the cart with the rest.

"You know I'm getting a picture of you wearing that for Nate, right?" EV snorted.

"What? Eww. Why did you have to put that in my head?"

"Just spreading the love. My work here is done."

Three days later, EV paced back and forth in front of six other shaggy, Ghillie-clad figures. Her volunteer Sasquatch army. The eighth would be joining them later. "You all know the plan, right? It's Foxes and Hounds with a twist. Be creative, have fun with it, but stay far enough ahead that they can only just catch you with their cameras. Be convincing and don't forget we need to get them to Big Hook Point, so remember that pace is everything."

"Most fun I've had in years." EV couldn't be sure, but she thought it was David Erickson who spoke.

Her phone beeped, and she fumbled her way through the strands of her costume to find it. A text from lookout Priscilla Lewellyn.

The game is afoot.

"Okay, it's on." She set the phone on vibrate, as planned, and slipped on her night-vision goggles. "It'll be about five minutes before they're in range. Can everyone see me?"

A chorus of yeses.

"Okay! Take your positions, and good luck, every-one." She moved to take her own.

The loud crack of a branch stopped the hunters in their tracks.

"Hear that? You see anything yet?"

They were aiming for a quiet passage, but when seven or eight people wearing heavy boots and carrying a bunch of camera equipment bungle their way through the woods, they make some noise.

"Use the night-vision glasses; they work better than the cams."

A pause. A rustle.

"Nothing. Keep going."

Ten feet away, dressed entirely in black, Horis snapped two more branches in rapid succession. When he heard the noise level rise among the hunters for a second time, he pitched his voice too low for them to hear and whispered, "Go for two." into the two-way radio headset he and his group of forest ninjas were using.

As planned, Sabra was not among the hunters. Deployed by EV, Talia and Lottie had fluttered into the midst of the hunter's camp, where Sabra was ensconced in a canvas chair drawn up to the fire. On cue, they started one of their famous arguments.

"You shouldn't be bothering them with that stupid picture, Lottie; it's nothing but a shadow."

"It is not. Look," Lottie gestured with her phone; the image on it had been staged by EV not half an hour before. "See, that's his head, and look—there's his arm. It's the Midnight Marauder."

"You're delusional." Talia sneaked a look out of the corner of her eye. The hunter she could see from where she was standing was on full alert. Time to push it home. "It's him. Shadows don't grunt. And I heard him breathing. I'm telling you, I think he's headed toward Big Hook Point."

"Why wouldn't he just take the trail, then?"

"Don't ask me, I'm not the expert. Here," she handed her phone to the scruffy, unwashed man sitting nearest her. He studied the photo for a few seconds.

"We got a live one."

"Can you show us where?" Dubicki spoke up.

"Sure. See. I told you they'd be interested." Lottie turned to Talia, away from where the hunters could see, waggled her eyebrows, and grinned.

Now for phase two.

Talia took the lead, setting the hunters on the right trail. When Sabra began to follow, Talia pulled her back. "Sabra, you have to come help me. I bought new curtains and the colors don't match. Can you help me?"

"But..."

"No, really. You have to come. They'll be fine without you. Please."

Before Sabra could pull away, the hunters were beyond hearing, and she was in Lottie's car, well on her way to Talia's house.

Since Foxes and Hounds was EV's game, she took the first leg of laying the trail. Slipping into an easy jog, she timed her passage through the trees perfectly, so the hunters could see flashes of her in the shaggy costume. Navigating through even light brush was difficult; nearly impossible. The Ghillie suit snagged too easily to let her stray from the main path.

This was why Horis and his team of black-clad forest ninjas were there: to provide ambiance. As EV passed, one of them rustled some bushes.

It was enough to keep the hunters engaged in the pursuit until they triggered the next phase.

EV put on speed, once she gained enough distance; she dodged left down a side trail while one of Horis' counterparts provided sound effects to cover her detour. She froze while another of her Sasquatch army, taking over for the next leg, drew the hunters out of hearing range.

Even with the night vision goggles, she didn't see Horis until he stepped up beside her. She stripped off the Ghillie suit and stuffed it out of sight. Underneath, she was dressed all in black. She would spend the rest of the evening slipping through the woods unseen.

"We good?" She took the headset and two-way radio he handed her.

"On schedule. Talia checked in. Sabra took the bait. Nate and Dalton are en route to the rendezvous point. I'm headed that way myself."

"Okay then. Time to ramp this thing up. I'll give the go ahead."

"Meet you in fifteen." Horis melted into the darkness without another sound—he moved like a cat through the woods.

EV keyed on the radio, "Go for phase three," she deployed three members of her Sasquatch army to double-team the hunters before slipping into the night, her long legs eating up the distance to the next rendezvous point.

Horis set a course adjacent to the hunter's path; directed his team; pitched in where needed. EV circled around to get in front of the action, while the group in costume led the hunters in circles.

"Omigod, there's two of them. You seeing what I'm seeing?" A hunter whispered in the darkness.

"What if it's a family? There might be babies. No one's ever caught footage of little ones."

"Shut up, they'll hear you."

"This is un-freaking-believable."Fifteen townspeople, plus Christian, followed Nate and Dalton down the main path toward Big Hook Point. EV would meet them any minute to guide Christian on ahead to where the final showdown would take place.

Whispered conversation covered up any sound she made, so when EV materialized in front of him, even though he expected her, Dalton jumped out of his skin.

"Here," she handed Dalton the headset she'd picked up from—well, she wasn't sure exactly who it was—but he or she had been at the rendezvous point, had handed EV the gear, and then dodged away toward the Point to complete final preparations. "Ten minutes, max. So step it up. On my mark, you all start making a big commotion. We need them to hear you before they see you." He doubted anyone else noticed the way her eyes avoided his, or the frosty edge to her tone.

"We'll be there." His tone neutral.

She turned to Nate, "Have you and Christian practiced your parts?" Chloe was in charge of the end game, and had given EV no more than a general idea of her plan.

"We're ready. It's going to be epic."

"Okay, see you all at the Point. Christian, let's go."

And she was gone again.

In hushed but reverent tones, the cameraman spoke fervently, "That's a family of four. Look at the two little ones. I think we've stumbled into a colony here. By my count, we've seen six, maybe seven altogether."

"You think they know we're following them? That last one was as big as a bear. What if they catch us? Maybe the reason no one ever gets this close is because when they do, they don't come back."

"I think we should call it a night. Can't we head back to camp now? We've taken enough footage already to score big. Let's go back." There was an edge of desperation to the words. The plan was working.

"Any of you think to grab the GPS? It feels like we've gone in circles. Unless we come out somewhere I recognize soon, I'm not even sure how to get back to camp." This from Dubicki who, despite his been-there-done-that attitude, had become a believer over the past couple hours.

"No, we're still in this. I need ten more minutes of footage." The one EV had dubbed 'Larry' brooked no refusal.

As the hunters moved off in the direction they'd last seen activity, they passed right by Horis and two of his cohorts. Horis used the noise of their passing as cover to relay, in a whisper, "Go for checkpoint five."

Sneaking through the wood in autumn would have been a much noisier prospect if they had not had the foresight to time this foray right after a good, soaking rain. Pine spills and wet leaves made for quieter movement.

Once the hunters passed out of hearing distance, Horis offered, "Our work here is done; you can head on home, or you can do what I'm doing and join the mob."

"No way I'm missing the show. I can't wait to see the looks on their faces."

"Let's go."

The three of them double-timed it to intercept the group of villagers before they made it to the Point.

Over the two-way com unit, Horis heard the countdown begin as hunters passed the final checkpoint.

From where she now sat, fifteen feet up in a tall pine tree, EV peered through a set of night-vision binoculars to locate the hunters. She didn't need the enhancement to see the torches carried by Nate and his group; those were visible to the naked eye. The two groups were about equal distance apart, and set to converge in the clearing below.

Christian stood, out of sight behind the same tree, waiting to join rest of the Ghillie-suited group. It wouldn't be long now.

When she judged they were close enough together, she gave the command to let Nate know it was time to make some noise. It all hinged on whether the hunters would run toward the sound, or away. If the former—it was game on, if the latter—all this work had been for nothing.

There was one moment where she held her breath as the hunters paused, but when they started moving forward again, she spoke the final command, "Radio silence in 3—2—1." She switched off her radio, shoved the headset into her pack, and scrambled back down from her perch.

When the hunters, the Sasquatch army, and the angry mob converged at the Point, EV was already in place.

She saw that Horis and his team, stripped of their unrelieved black, were now mingled in with Nate's group. It was time for the show.

"There they are. Get them." Someone from the torch-lit group shouted, when the flickering flames revealed the shaggy figures. Quickly, the towns-people surrounded the erstwhile group of Sasquatches—the light from their torches adding drama to the staged setting.

Chloe had worked a miracle. Her subtle makeup effects—shadowing around the eyes and cheeks—made the angry mob look even more formidable. More stunning, though, was what she had done with the Sasquatch family. She'd cut the hoods off the Ghillie suits so their faces showed, and then, skill-fully, applied facial hair and makeup to complete the transformation. EV had expected to see her there among the crowd, but so far, Chloe was not in evidence.

EV had organized the lead-up, but this final show—well, this was all Chloe.

"No. Stop." A Yeti hunter, one of the females, called out with an impassioned plea, "They're a gentle people. Don't hurt them."

"They're thieves, and they deserve what's coming to them." Dalton growled. "They've terrorized our town and now they have to pay." A general roar of agreement rose from the angry mob, who brandished their torches and pitchforks.

EV bit her lip to keep from laughing out loud at the looks of consternation on the hunter's faces, which were clearly picked out by the light of the torches.

Christian shuffled forward, grunting and raising his arms as though trying to communicate with the armed villagers. His posture could be mistaken either for aggression, or an attempt at forming a truce.

A chant arose from the crowd, "Get him! Get him!"

Nate brandished the pitchfork at Christian, who redoubled his efforts, and before the hunters could intervene, a ring of townspeople hemmed them in so they could do nothing but watch, horrified, as Nate took another swipe with the weapon.

The villagers continued to chant; Nate squared off against Christian, feinting and thrusting with the fork until they had maneuvered themselves into exactly the right position. With a barely perceptible nod, Nate lunged. The fork pierced Christian through the chest, and then withdrew, covered with blood.

It looked real enough that EV shuddered, even though she knew the pitchfork's tines had retracted into a cavity filled with fake blood, before popping back out to drip realistically.

One of the hunters slumped over.

But the worst was yet to come.

As though in a bloodlust frenzy, the townspeople went to work on the rest of the hairy family. Soon, even the Sasquatch children—Veronica's two eldest—lay dead on the ground, while the hunters looked on in utter shock.

The shock turned to fear, though, when Nate cast an appraising eye over them. "What should we do with this bunch? Can't have any witnesses."

Already pale faces blanched to deadly white.

"You can't."

"No! Please, I have a family."

"Omigod! Look!"

A ghostly figure rose from the darkness to hover above the ground.

EV put her hand to her mouth to stifle the giggles. It was Chloe in that damned Yeti suit, and she'd done something to it to make it glow. From her position, EV could see the two black-suited figures holding Chloe up by her legs, but she'd bet anything they were invisible from where the hunters huddled.

"I am the ghost of…." Chloe intoned, then paused.

The group of hunters stood, transfixed, waiting for her to continue.

"Put me down." Chloe spoke in her normal voice. Once on the ground, she pulled off the Ghillie suit hood to reveal her own normal features, and strode over to where the hunters stood with mouths hanging open. "Exactly how stupid are you people?"

Before anyone could answer, she broke into a patented Chloe-rant. "You show up here uninvited, invade our privacy, and generally wreak havoc for what? Fame and fortune? What is it that goes on in your little pea brains that makes you think you're entitled to do whatever it is that you want?"

Dubicki was the first to catch on. The others didn't understand until the dead Sasquatch family began to rise from the ground.

"This was all a hoax? There was never a sighting? You people have been stringing us along for weeks."

"Tonight was a prank. Happy Halloween, and welcome to our version of a haunted hayride. And if you thought there was a sighting, it was all in your tiny minds. I repeat. NO ONE INVITED YOU TO COME HERE. You did that of your own accord, and we figured the only way to get rid of you was to give you what you came for. Now, you have a choice, you can pack up and get out of town tonight, or we can press charges against you for trespassing, since you're currently standing right in the middle of posted land."

"Maybe it's us who should press charges."

"For what? None of you has been harmed, and I don't think there's a law against scaring people. Nate, you want to back me up on that?"

"She's right. You came here willingly. You're trespassing on private land. I know the owner's around here somewhere. EV, where are you?"

"Right here." EV pulled off her mask and stepped forward. "I'll decline to press charges as long as you all promise you'll be gone by morning."

"Okay—okay, we'll go, but just out of curiosity, can you tell us about the image Mrs. Pruitt posted online? I'd like to hear the story."

"It was me," Christian stepped forward. "A misunderstanding. I was lost in the woods, but now, I'm home."

Chapter 29

The Sasq-Watchers kept their word. By the next morning, they'd gone; leaving behind a field full of litter and a demoralized Sabra, who had gotten caught up in the buzz. A rumor hit the grapevine that Jim Dubicki wanted to stay with Lottie, but she turned him down.

Christian planned to stay on for a while, even after his parents left for home. In the meantime, they were spending one week at each of the inns. They were a lovely family. If EV had to predict, Chris would become a permanent Pines resident.

The final blip left on her radar was the blackmail plot she wanted to unravel, and the single lead she had was the sneaking suspicion her ex was involved. Worse, she was sure Dalton had information on that front, and right now, the two of them were barely speaking.

And that was another situation she needed to deal with. But not today. Today she had work to do.

EV hiked down the path toward the fairy garden carrying a large plastic tote. Winterizing the fairy garden always made her feel a little sad. She'd already made several trips back and forth from the truck, hauling in a series of wooden windbreaks that reminded her of folded easels. On the trip to the garden, the tote held burlap, canvas, and twine she would use to wrap some of the larger decorations; on its return trip, it would carry away the smaller, more fragile winged sprites who would wait out the fierce winds of winter cocooned in her garage.

She made a lovely picture there, surrounded by whimsy, when Dalton happened upon her. Lost in thought, she hadn't heard him coming.

"We need to talk."

She jumped a little when he spoke. "Deja Vu," she said.

In spite of himself, he smiled. "Actually, I need to talk." The smile fell away to reveal frustration. "Except I'm not sure what to say."

EV lost her breath. She knew where this was headed without him saying another word.

"Before we get into all that, do you have evidence

to prove Remy Vincent was behind the blackmail attempt on Evan Plunkett?" She took a page from his book and changed the subject to her ex.

"I..." He tried to dodge, but the truth flashed across his face. "How did you figure it out?"

"Seriously? You brought him up time after time. It was either jealousy—which after baring my soul, you should have known wasn't a factor—or you found out something about him that might be upsetting to me."

"It's uncanny how you always figure things out."

"You should also know that he spoke to Lila about me a few weeks ago."

"Well, if I'd known that, jealousy might have been a stronger possibility. What did he want?" Dalton's nostrils flared, but that was the single outward sign that he was furious.

"Nothing specific. He gave her the shifty vibe, so she called to let me know. I would have told you about it then, if you hadn't been trying to keep things from me."

"Are you sure about that? You're the champion of keeping secrets."

The way he said it, with such dry derision, cut EV to the bone.

"Whatever you may think, Dalton Burnsoll, a few dates, and a roll in the hay doesn't give you the right to know every tiny detail of my life. I trusted you with the most painful thing in my past."

"I didn't mean…I was talking about the way you and Chloe worked together when Evan died, and again to find Christian." Still, he could see why she misinterpreted what he'd said.

They were going in circles again.

"What was all you wanted to tell me?"

"What?" The conversation had gone so far off topic he had to snap his mind back to remember what it was he meant to say. Once he did, he discovered the desire to define their relationship had gone.

His muttered *nothing* wasn't convincing at all. He'd come here to clear the tension; to tell her how he felt about her. She'd thrown him for a loop with knowing Vincent's connection to the blackmail scheme.

EV sighed. "I called you as soon as I knew where to find Christian, and I've already told you the Ashton thing happened way too fast. Neither of those things holds a candle to what you were hiding from me."

"I was just doing my job."

Stalling for time, EV fed another fairy into the tote. "Where does that leave us?"

He wanted her more than ever, but Remy Vincent stood between them as surely as if he were physically still in her life. "Where do you think we are?" Dalton countered. He gently reached out; grasped her shoulders; turned her to face him.

There was a vulnerability about her he'd never seen before. "I...I have feelings for you." She bit down on the word *love* before it crossed her lips. "What we have seems worth exploring..."

"But," he finished for her, "You need to put your past with Remy fully to rest."

How could he understand her so well? No one else besides Chloe ever had.

"Will you let me help you put him away? Then we can move forward with nothing more standing in the way?" It surprised her how much she wanted him.

His answer came in the form of a kiss that held more than a promise of the passion he felt.

"Let's get this done. I've waited for you long enough, Emmalina Valentina Torrence."

Chapter 30

Nate sat in a camp chair on the back deck of his father's house, a small fire burning in the pit in front of him. Every few minutes, poked at the coals or added another piece of wood absentmindedly. His body was moving, but his mind was somewhere else; with someone else.

"You need to separate those logs a little; let some air in, or you'll stifle the flame." Martin Harper had emerged from inside and watched his son's expression as he stared into the flames. "Do you want to talk about it?" He asked, knowing full well what was the subject matter of Nate's recent funk. His son was preoccupied, and Martin hoped he would open up and find a happy resolution.

Silence stretched between them for several minutes before Nate finally asked, "What made you want to stay here in the Pines when Mom wanted to go chasing a lucrative career in Portland?"

Martin leaned forward, elbows resting on his knees; in profile, he and Nate resembled one another so closely that if Martin's salt-and-pepper hair were not visible, it would be difficult to tell the two apart from even a short distance. "I didn't want to leave because you loved it here so much. It wasn't until you were a teenager that you felt the pull of the world outside this forest. You enjoyed helping me tend the gardens; you worked in the community, and even told me you wanted to become a Selectman someday."

"Really? I don't remember that." Nate searched his brain for the trigger that pushed him to want to leave and start a new life outside the confines of home. He recalled one summer, when Chloe had come to visit for a few weeks. They were about 16, and she had just come back from a trip to Costa Rica. While she regaled him with stories from her travels, he had felt his confidence shrinking until it lay curled in a fetal position on the floor of his mind. She had blossomed in the two years since he had last seen her: no more awkward elbows and knees; just bright eyes and wavy blond hair he wanted to run his fingers through.

Rather than act on his true feelings, Nate wimped out again, even when the perfect opportunity to sweep her off her feet fell into his lap. Walking her home after watching some chick flick together, Chloe made a remark about how your soul mate could be your best friend and you might never realize it.

The next thing he knew, he was standing in the fairy garden—a section of forest trail decorated with twinkly lights and hundreds of fairy figurines—looking down at Chloe, and knowing she expected him to kiss her in order to test the theory. His past experience—all of five minutes spent in a closet with Jessica Donato the winter before—was not going to help him here.

Heart pounding so loudly she must be able to hear it, he had looked into her eyes—fallen into them was probably more accurate—and seen his future. Wanting this moment to stretch out forever, but needing it to end before it killed him, he bent down to touch his lips to hers. Smelling like candy and shampoo, she leaned closer; her eyes fluttered shut.

Out of nowhere, nervous laughter bubbled up just as his lips touched hers; she giggled too, and the moment was lost. By the time they emerged from the woods, Nate had managed to cover his disappointment enough to say goodnight. Feeling pathetic, he stomped home to relieve the frustration by punching his pillow.

That's when Nate's attitude about the Pines shifted. He wanted to feel he was good enough for Chloe, and he figured she needed someone who had as much worldly experience as she did. After a while, he resigned himself to the fact that she would probably wander the globe forever; and though he had done his fair share of traveling, it wasn't a life he wanted in the long-term. So, he turned to his career for fulfillment, and spent his off time pursuing a series of ill-fated relationships. Nobody would ever live up to his ideal, and he had started to think he would be a bachelor forever.

Worse, he had created an association between the pain of loving Chloe and his hometown.

Nate's epiphany happened over only a few moments, but suddenly he was thinking clearly. "Thanks, Dad." He bolted through the back door and through the house while Martin stared after him. "You're welcome. I guess."

Chloe had barely settled onto the couch with a cup of tea and a book, Sugar and Spice curled up at her feet, when she heard the front door open. *Great, she thought, I was hoping for a quiet evening. Hasn't there been enough craziness for one week?* "Who's there?" She called out loud. As though they knew someone they liked was at the door, the kittens ears perked and they sprinted toward the entryway.

Before she could untangle herself from the chenille blanket covering her legs, Nate burst into the living room, Sugar purring contentedly in his arms and Spice hanging from his pants as she tried to claw her way up his body. He tried to set Sugar down on the floor, but she leapt back into his arms, so Nate sat down on the other end of the couch and let both cats rub against him.

"Can we talk, please?" He directed at Chloe, who was, at this point, dealing with a number of emotions: surprise, curiosity, hope, nervousness, and a fascination with his fingers as they stroked tawny fur.

"So talk." She retorted, unwilling to break until she knew exactly what had brought him here.

"I'm not dating Elise. She's a private investigator

who's been helping with the blackmail case. I didn't tell you, at first, because the town elders closed the investigation, and I was trying to keep things quiet."

He squirmed a moment, then stood to remove a handful of cat toys he hadn't noticed until he was sitting on them. Framing his next admission, he tossed a fuzzy mouse toward the kitchen; smiling when two lithe bodies scrambled for the toy.

The rest of his confession came in a rush, "After that, I didn't tell you because it seemed to bother you so much, and I was mad at you for dating when I thought we were both on the same page. I've wanted to tell you how I feel for a long time; longer than you even realize. When you moved back, I thought you'd stay for a bit and take off; I didn't want to get involved and have you leave again. But you're not leaving, and neither am I. I'm moving back to the Pines for good, Chloe. And I've loved you since we were kids."

Before Nate could continue, Chloe launched herself onto his lap and planted a kiss square on his lips. Nate wrapped his arms around her as the kiss slowed and deepened; he stroked her back, ran his fingers through her silky hair. She tasted like spring water: clean, and fresh, and deeply satisfying. The touch of his strong hands caressing her skin so gently made her hungry for more. Her own fingers tangled in his hair, down broad, muscular shoulders, and came to rest on his chest as she pulled away, with effort, to stare into Nate's glowing eyes.

"I love you, too. And I'm here, for keeps. I'm yours; I think I always have been." His mouth found hers again. This time, the kiss ran even deeper than before, and both Chloe and Nate lost themselves in the moment. Joy and desire rolled off them as they clung to one another. Details could be discussed later; they had all the time in the world, now that they were where they were supposed to be.

Thanks for reading! We know you're wondering what will happen next in Ponderosa Pines.

Keep reading for a preview of Caught in the Frame, where Chloe and EV travel to Ireland for Chloe's mother's wedding—where, of course, there's a mystery to solve!

Quick Author's Note

If you weren't already aware, ReGina and Erin are a mother/daughter writing team, and yes, that means we mix family and work - with all the ups and downs you might expect. It helps that we basically share a single brain most of the time and tend to finish each other's sentences...literally. It also means we sometimes squabble over plot points, but since we're best friends, too, we let that stuff roll right off our backs.

This is the first series we ever wrote together, and it holds a special place in our hearts. Fun fact! In the book, the town's name of Ponderosa Pines came about as a compromise between the couple who founded the town. In reality, it came from the name of the apartment building Erin was living in at the time!

We intended to set the story in a similar apartment complex but as things went along, we ended with something just a bit quirkier. Ponderosa Pines is a place we'd both like to live.

In case you're wondering how we split up the work when we write together, we come up with a plot and scene list and then call dibs on which ones we want to write. In this case, Erin called all of the Chloe scenes while ReGina handled EV. As always, we go over each other's work once the book is done.

Anyway, if you've come this far with us and not decided we're complete and total whackadoodles… and especially if you have, we're offering a chance to sign up for our newsletters— the best place to get new release updates, sales notifications, and other fun content.

You can sign up for ReGina's newsletter here and/or Erin's newsletter here. As a thank-you gift for hanging out with us, you'll also get a FREE novella that isn't available anywhere else. And of course, we promise not to SPAM your inbox!

Love, hugs, and happy reading,
ReGina & Erin

P.S. If you enjoyed this book, it would be great if you

could leave a review or recommendation on your favorite store, GoodReads, or BookBub.

Your reviews help indie authors sell more books!

PONDEROSA PINES
MYSTERIES - BOOK THREE

"... **A**nd then he kissed me." Chloe LaRue paused for dramatic effect, remembering the way Nathaniel Harper's hands had tangled in her hair; the love that poured from his lips and sent her senses reeling. Twin sighs escaped the mouths of her two girlfriends, Veronica and Mindy, as they listened with rapt attention. Chloe relished the rare chance to gush about her up-until-recently non-existent love life.

A large pizza, so far untouched, rested on the coffee table, surrounded by an array of snacks that, if polished off in one night, would send all three of them into total sugar shock. Veronica sipped a bright pink cocktail through a makeshift Twizzler straw, her cornflower blue eyes opening wide over the rim as she absorbed every word of Chloe's story. Mindy sat stick-straight in a lotus position, her feet tangled, pretzel-like, in front of her. Chloe and Veronica were so used to the yoga instructor's mannerisms they barely noticed anymore when Mindy twisted herself into spontaneous poses at the oddest of times.

"What happened next?" Veronica wiggled her eyebrows suggestively, correctly deciphering the blush rising to stain Chloe's cheeks a delicate pink. She wouldn't—couldn't—let it go without ribbing her friend just a bit. After watching Nate and Chloe engage in a two-decade-long mating dance they had nicknamed the Will They, Won't They Waltz, Veronica and Mindy were delighted the pair had finally realized their true feelings for one another.

Pining for each other since puberty—but having lived most of that time on opposite corners of the world—the two of them had now permanently returned to the tiny town of Ponderosa Pines, making a long term relationship possible. However, miscommunication and a healthy dose of insecurity made the transition from *friends* to *more than friends* difficult, to say the least.

Chloe rolled her eyes and raised her right eyebrow at Veronica, shooting her friend a glance correctly interpreted as "Duh", and continued. "I haven't had enough of these to go into the gory details," she raised her glass for emphasis, "and I don't intend to. But, we definitely took our relationship to the next level. A couple of times." Chloe grinned sheepishly, and her friends dissolved into giggles.

Three short days ago, Nate had burst through her front door to officially declare his love. Chloe would have been quite content to continue spending every possible second since then devoted to memorizing the long lines of his spectacular body. Instead, reality and responsibility pried them out of their love nest, and forced Nate back to his assignment of training Ponderosa Pines' newest lawman. Rather than sit around and wait for him, Chloe had turned her phone back on, answered the dozen or so messages that had accrued on her voicemail, and acquiesced to an impromptu girls' night in.

As the last—or second-to-last, if you counted her very closest friend, EV Torrence—one of the group to lose her single status, Chloe couldn't deny the desire to *tell* someone about the incredible weekend she had just experienced. So what if they were all thirty-something, and probably too old to be giggling like school girls; you were only as old as you felt, and it still made them all happy to act like teenagers every once in a while.

Veronica, whose near-perfect marriage produced five beautiful, rambunctious children—and Mindy, childless by choice, but very much in love with her longtime boyfriend—were over the moon about the recent development in Chloe and Nate's relationship. Now, if only EV could sort out her own love life, all of Chloe's closest friends would be coupled up. Of course, EV had twenty years on the rest of them, so her situation was a bit more complicated than the others.

"You two can pull those canary feathers out of your mouths, by the way. EV already told me you were in on her little plot. Dragging me into situations where I'd have to see Nate was bad enough, but setting me up to date a bunch of losers and make Nate look like the better choice...jerks." Her grin showed she bore no malice. "I already knew he was perfect, I just let fear get the best of me."

"Should we expect retaliation?" Veronica smirked. "What you did to EV wasn't so different from what we did to you, Miss Pot Who Calls Kettles Black."

Chloe had to admit submitting her best friend's

profile to an online dating service probably went a bit beyond nice. Yet, she defended herself, "As if EV's one to talk. She and Dalton are perfect for each other, and you can tell he's totally in love with her. Too bad she's still holding him at arm's length."

"That's not what I heard!" Mindy sing-songed. "There's a rumor going around that he was seen leaving her house after a torrid night of lust—at least that's what Lottie Calabrese's been telling everyone. Care to confirm?"

Chloe rolled her eyes but conceded, "Yes, it's true. But they hit another bump in the road, and still have a few issues to work out." How much should she tell them about recent developments?

Almost no one knew that former resident, Remy Vincent—who just happened to also be EV's ex—was suspect number one in Ponderosa Pines' first mystery of note. Unless the evidence lied, Remy had master-minded an attempted coup that would have forced their beloved town into being dissolved and absorbed by neighboring Gilmore. Remy's blackmail attempt failed miserably when its victim, Evan Plunkett, turned up dead—murdered by the cuckolded husband of Evan's most recent paramour. Everyone knew that part of the story—just not that the shadowy figure attempting to play puppet-master with their town had such close ties. Until Remy was caught, EV and Dalton had agreed to put their budding relationship on hold—a decision Chloe thought bordered on the ridiculous. So what if Dalton's job as deputy meant he had to keep certain bits of evidence from EV? It wasn't like she told him everything either.

"I have every intention of lending a hand; what's good for the goose is good for the gander."

"Lending a hand?" Mindy practically snorted out the words. "You mean meddling in their business."

Chloe put on her best innocent look—Bambi eyes and all. "It's done out of love."

If EV had been completely happy as a vibrant, single woman, Chloe would have let the topic drop. And, until a recently-single Dalton came into the picture, a series of short-term relationships satisfied EV's occasional craving for companionship. Enter Nate's partner, the caring Deputy Dalton, and every-thing changed. For the first time since the disaster of Remy, EV let someone into her life who might just become permanent.

Unfortunately, Remy Vincent still stood between them. Suspecting she was at the heart of his vendetta against Ponderosa Pines, EV had pulled back from the relationship with Dalton. Until all that was laid to rest, they were in a holding pattern. Chloe sighed to herself, hoping silently that everything would work out in the end, and pushed the thought from her mind in order to focus on more pleasant matters

Caught in the Frame is available now, and keep reading for a preview of the free novella you'll get for joining our newsletters.

A Free Story for You

Enjoyed meeting Chloe & EV? They're not the only people who live in our heads!

Sign up for either or both of our newsletters and you'll receive *A Snowball's Chance in Spell*, a prequel novella featuring characters from the *Mag & Clara Balefire Mysteries*, the *Haunted Everly After Mysteries*, and the *Psychic Seasons* series.

Christmas is canceled! Lexi Balefire's faerie godmothers didn't mean to knock Santa Claus and his sleigh out of the sky, but now his reindeer are missing, and it's up to Lexi to find them all before time runs out and Christmas is ruined!

Excerpt from A Snowball's Chance in Spell

Lightning flirted in shadows of the dark clouds hovering over my house when I came home from work the afternoon before my twenty-second Christmas Eve. Nothing unusual there. With three elemental faeries living in the house, weird weather happened all the time. Or rather, every time my temperamental godmothers mounted some sort of snit.

The godmothers idled at snit.

Going back to work wasn't an option. I'd cleared the last match of the year—a lovely couple with a shared affection for online gaming—and I was no coward. When it came to diffusing faerie fights, I consider myself an expert, and this one didn't look like it rated more than a two on the volcano scale.

Yes, you heard right. I measure faerie fights on the scale of whether or not a volcano might erupt in my backyard. Living with faeries is never boring. Occasionally dangerous—especially because I have yet to come into the magic that is my birthright, but never boring.

A quick check proved they'd contained the madness to the inside and/or the backyard. The two feet of snow on the front lawn was still there and still white—you try explaining black snow to your neighbors sometime. I didn't see any winged denizens—fae or otherwise—dotting the roof ridge, or hear any ominous sounds. If not for the fact that lightning is rare in Maine during the winter, and rarer still when confined to a single area, I'd have thought it was a quiet day in the household.

In my head, I downgraded the threat to a level one, and went inside.

For the most part, my place looks like an ordinary, New England style home. Built by my great grandparents, it's the oldest house in a neighborhood that grew up around it when the suburbs expanded into what was once a rural area. Because, I think, the faeries wanted to give me a normal upbringing, they left the house in mostly the same condition it was in when they came to take care of me and only added on a wing for their own use.

I stepped into the front hall expecting...well, just about anything. Did I mention the faeries love holidays? Maybe they don't have them in the faelands, or maybe they do and go overboard there, too. I can't say since I've never been, but I could tell at a glance there were more decorations than there had been when I left.

"Terra!" I yelled, but got no answer. Terra, faerie of earth, held sway over all the flora and fauna found on dry land. She would be the one responsible for the pine boughs twining over anything that held still long enough. Fire faerie, Soleil, contributed by setting sparks of faerie light to twinkle inside the delicate ice bubbles crafted by her sister, Evian, mistress of water. The effect was lovely, but not as lovely as the three women could be when their faces weren't twisted, as they were now, with rage.

I came upon them in their favorite fighting grounds: the kitchen. It looked like I'd caught this one early since there was relatively little damage done so far. Steam rose from a puddle of water at Soleil's feet which I assumed had come from Evian. Vines snaked from between the kitchen tiles to twine around Evian's ankles, and there were a few smoking embers dotting Terra's hair. Nothing more than a minor spat.

Keeping it casual, I asked, "What's going on?"

There's no rhyme or reason to what will settle a fight or send one into the red zone.

Terra turned one granite pink eye in my direction. "This doesn't concern you." The fingers of her left hand twitched and the vines slithered from Evian's ankles to her knees.

Retaliating, Evian conjured a gush of water from thin air, and doused the smoking embers. The scent of pine boughs couldn't compete with the stench of burnt hair, or the pungent funk erupting from the flowers that burst into bloom near her feet.

"Now look," I pointed out to Terra before she conjured something worse. "Evian is trying to help."

"Was not." Evian snapped her fingers and turned Terra's wet hair white with frost, except because the vines were now questing higher, she overshot the mark and doused a few of Soleil's decorative sparkles.

That was the moment I lost control.

Oh, who am I kidding? I never had control.

Soleil let out a screech and lobbed a fireball at Evian, who encased it in a ball of water and batted it toward Terra. I felt scoured clean when Terra called all the dirt and dust in the house to form a layer over the bobbing ball of doom which now resembled a small planet whizzing back toward Soleil.

It might have ended better if I'd have kept my mouth shut, but I didn't.

"You're going to put an eye out with that thing."

The ire of three faeries is a potent thing, but not as potent as a flaming mudball. I ducked, rolled, and hit the latch on the patio door in what I'd like to think was a graceful move. Probably looked like a seal rolling off a rock.

The flaming fireball arced over my head, its warm breeze tossing my hair, and rocketed off into the sky.

Crisis averted. Except, it wasn't. I should have known.

A Snowball's Chance in Spell is only available by signing up for one of our newsletters here:
https://reginawelling.com
https://erinlynnwrites.com

Other Books

If you'd like to meet more people who live rent-free in our heads, here's a list of other series we've written. Our books are all set in fictional towns in Maine, and some characters like to flit back and forth between series. The cast of Psychic Seasons hangs out with Everly and also with Lexi Balefire from the Fate Weaver series. Mag and Clara Balefire are Lexi's grandmother and aunt!

The Psychic Seasons Series
Four women, four love stories, and a whole lot of supernatural surprises. In the quaint town of Oakville, Maine, psychic visions, ghostly whispers, and fate itself conspire to change lives—and hearts—forever

The Haunted Everly After Mysteries

Everly Dupree came home for a fresh start—not a full-time gig solving ghostly murders. But when the dearly departed start demanding justice, what's a reluctant medium to do?

Nell Page: Accidental Investigator
Nell Page owns a bookstore, drinks too much coffee, and has a habit of noticing things she probably shouldn't. With warmth, wit, and an accidental talent for investigating, Nell tackles mysteries that don't always involve murder—but always matter.

Fate Weaver
Lexi Balefire—matchmaker, witch, and accidental fate-weaver—must balance love, magic, and a family legacy of chaos before destiny decides for her!

The Mag and Clara Balefire Mysteries
Sister witches Mag and Clara Balefire move to a sleepy Maine town for a fresh start—only to find themselves conjuring up trouble, solving murders, and keeping their magic under wraps in this charmingly witchy cozy mystery series

Laurel Haven Witches
Four witches, destined by blood and magic, must embrace their power, battle a dark legacy, and surrender to the love that could break the curse—or bind them to it forever.

www.ingramcontent.com/pod-product-compliance
Lightning Source LLC
Chambersburg PA
CBHW061640190726
48289CB00006B/1676